falling for AGENT CRUZ

Nothing is as it seems

A Falling novel
by DL Gallie

There's no rhyme or reason when it comes to happily ever afters.
Falling in love happens when you least expect it.

CHARLI
I was betrayed, now I don't trust easily.
One night I let loose and do something crazy.
When my new partner is assigned, I'm shocked to find we've already met.
From the moment my eyes land on him, again, I know I'm screwed.
Dominic Cruz crashes through my fortress and I start to trust again.
Until I don't.
Things happen that will once again change me, and every-thing I thought I knew.

DOMINIC
This new assignment fell into my lap.
I was reluctant but then I met my new partner—Charli Davis.
The one who rocked my world and left in the morning.
Our connection was instant and it's still as intense.
My future is finally looking bright.
Then the past reappears.
Now everything is uncertain, but nothing is as it seems.

Published by DL Gallie Author

First published 3rd February 2021

Cover designed by **Kristy**, Vanilla Lilly Designs

Edited by **Karen Hrdlicka**, Barren Acres Editing

Proofread by **Gemma,** Gem's Precise Proofreading

Formatting and interior design by **DL Gallie**

ALSO BY DL GALLIE

STAND ALONES

Out of Nowhere

Antecedent

Seven Nights

Doc Steel

Christmas Treats

Oops

Fractured:A driven world novel - coming mid 2021

IPHTILY - coming late 2021

In the Dark of Night anthology**

Secrets anthology**

***only available in paperback direct from me*

FALLING NOVELS

Falling for Dr. Kelly

Falling for Dr. Knight

Falling for Agent Cox

Falling for Agent Cruz

THE UNEXPECTED SERIES

When it comes to love, expect the unexpected

The Unexpected Gift

The Unexpected Letter

The Unexpected Package

The Unexpected Connection

THE CASTAWAY GROVE COLLECTION

Love has arrived in the Grove

Oasis

Unequivocal Love

Five Words

Broken Rules

…and a few more to come.

The Castaway Grove Collection, books 1- 4

THE LIQUOR CABINET SERIES

Liquor has never been so disturbingly saucy

Malt Me (Book 1)

Tequila Healing (Book 2)

Wine Not (Book 3)

The Final Shot (Book 4)

The Liquor Cabinet: Series boxset

To my Henchwench, Tara
Thank you for being my wench XoXoX

There is never a time or place for true love. It happens accidentally, in a heartbeat, in a single flashing, throbbing moment.

~ *Sarah Dessen*

PROLOGUE

BETRAYAL.

Verb.

To fail or desert especially in time of need…and for the second time in as many months, I've been betrayed. Once again, someone close has let me down. This time it hurts so much more because the person who betrayed me is also the man who stole my heart.

I knew he was too good to be true and rather than listening to my head, I listened to my traitorous vagina and heart. *Assholes*. Now, my life is in the toilet—like my head currently—but this time, I have more than myself to think about. All I want to do is crawl into a ball, drink myself into oblivion, and eat my weight in Doritos, but I can't. I have to be strong because people are relying on me, but just once, I'd love for someone to look after me.

Sitting up, I rest my back against the tub and stare into nothing. "Stronger" by Britney Spears starts playing from the living room and as I listen to the words, they hit me hard.

Standing up, I stare at my reflection in the guest room's mirror and decide that yes, I am strong. I can do this, alone. No more wallowing. I will not let a penis ruin my life. I'm Charli fucking Davis, kick-ass agent...and soon-to-be mom.

CHARLI 1

...ten weeks earlier

"...HE'S DIRTY, CHARLI," AMANDA, THE BOSS, TELLS ME.

"Come again?" I question, but I'm already processing what she just told me and deep down I know everything she said is in fact one-hundred-percent correct.

"Dean is working for Vlahos. He was responsible for the explosion that took out Corey's car. Bomb making pieces, similar to what forensics retrieved, were found in his apartment."

"That's pretty dumb of him."

"I'd guess that when he failed to take Corey out, he was rocked and skittish. From memory, you guys moved to the cabin straight after the attempt. He clearly didn't have time to clean up his mess."

Shaking my head in disbelief, I rub my forehead. "So what do we do now?"

"A team will return with you now and try to catch him in the act."

"He'll be suspicious if I return with backup."

"Which is why we will have a cover story stating that another threat has been made against Cox and since he's a fellow agent, everything is being done to keep him safe."

"That will work. Will they return with me? Or come up later?"

"Both. Agent Barber will return with you now to have an extra set of eyes and ears inside. Agents Isaac, Jenkins, Drake, and Thorpe will be on stakeout, they are all set to go once we've formulated everything. Charli, it's imperative that Dean doesn't know about this."

"I won't be letting anything on. I want to take him down as much as you do. I'm just pissed I didn't put two and two together. I knew something was amiss with him, but I just thought it was his hatred toward Cox affecting him."

"Don't beat yourself up over this."

"Easier said than done," I tell her. Some agent I am, I didn't even realize that my partner is dirty.

"Davis," Amanda snaps, "I need your head in the game."

"I'll be fine, Boss."

"Good," she says and she leaves my office.

Leaning back in my chair, I stare at the ceiling, frustrated with myself. I'm an agent, a federal fucking agent, and I missed all the signs pointing to my partner being a corrupt asshole. I should've known something was up with Dean, but he played me like a fool. However, I will have the last laugh. I will do everything in my power to bring him and Vlahos to justice.

Grabbing the file Amanda left, I go over all that she has

and I add my suggestions and notes for how to proceed from here. By the time I have the plan amended, it's early in the morning. I should be sleeping but I'm running on adrenalin, caffeine—a lot of caffeine—and anger right now.

A knock on my door, startles me. I was so lost in my head, I didn't hear my name being called. "Davis, we are ready to finalize the plan," Agent Barber tells me.

"Thanks, Bec," I respond.

Standing up, I follow her down to the conference room. Everyone falls silent when we walk in. I pause at the entrance to the room and they all stare at me. I hate the look of pity reflecting in their eyes. "Okay, yep, this sucks. I don't want to hear 'sorry' or anything along those lines. All I want to do is bring him to justice and put Vlahos back where he belongs. If you have a problem with that, there's the door." I point behind me. No one moves or utters a word. You could hear a pin drop in here. "I'll take the silence as we are good."

Stepping into the room, I close the door behind me and take a seat. "Okay, here's the plan."

Exactly thirty minutes later, Bec and I are in my car and on our way back to the cabin. The others will follow and get to their tasks while we get to ours.

"I know you said to not say anything, but since I'll be living with you for the foreseeable future, I feel I have like a roommate privilege." I laugh at this. "How are you doing with all this?"

"I feel like a fool. I'm a federal fucking agent and I didn't see what was happening right under my nose."

"He had everyone fooled, Charli."

"Yeah, but I'm his partner. I've been living with him for the last few weeks and I didn't suspect a thing. He was doing all of this right under my nose. He and Vlahos must be laughing at me and my ignorance."

"And that will play perfectly into this. His cocky ass won't see us coming."

"I hope you're right, Bec."

The sun has been up for about an hour when we reach the cabin. As we approach, I notice a car in the driveway and my senses tell me something is up. Immediately, I'm on high alert and pull to the side of the road. Without saying a word, Bec grabs her phone and calls the office for a plate check. It comes back registered to a Dr. Monica Quinn.

"Fuck," I scoff. "He's here." Looking to Bec, I order her, "Call the other team and tell them to get here ASAP, I'm going to go in."

"Alone?" she questions.

"Yep, I'm meant to be there so they won't suspect anything if I'm caught walking in. They won't expect me to have backup so we have an element of surprise, even if I'm discovered."

"Be careful," she reminds me.

Nodding my head, I reach over to the glove compartment and grab my gun. Climbing out of the car, I slip the weapon into the waistband of my jeans. Once it's secured, I make my way over to the cabin.

Ducking by Monica's car, I hear voices coming from around the back. Sneaking onto the property, I press myself to the side of the cabin and slink around the side. Ducking below the deck, I move farther into the yard. Peeking under the railing, my eyes widen at the scene before me.

Corey and Avery Evans are bound and on opposite sides of the deck. Monica Quinn, Dean, and Vlahos are standing around. Dean startles and trips on his deceptive fat feet and knocks over the trash can on the deck. The loud noise echoes in the quiet of the morning, "You alright there, heffalump?" Vlahos spits at Dean.

"There was a bug," he whines, this causes Corey to laugh and it pisses Dean off. He storms and punches Corey a few times, pushing him to the deck. "You're a dead man, Cox," he snarls at a beaten and bloody Corey.

"Enough," Vlahos bellows. Then from inside we hear Baylor yell for Cox. A sinister smile appears on Vlahos's face, "It's go time."

"Shit," I mumble, I was hoping backup would be here before this happened. Kye grabs and roughly manhandles a quivering, and visibly shaken, Avery inside. Cox spots me and I mouth, 'Backup is on the way' but before he can acknowledge me, the kitchen door swings open again.

Dropping down out of sight, I sneak another look and see Kye step back out onto the deck, pushing Avery and Baylor in front of him. I shake my head when I realize that he's using them as a shield. He really is a piece of work.

Cox laughs and everyone turns their heads to face him. "What the fuck are you laughing at, asshole?" Dean growls.

"Big bad Kye Vlahos is using two women as a shield. He's a fucking pansy." *You dickhead*, I think to myself, typical macho man trying to show off in front of his woman. From the corner of my eye, I see Bec and backup on the street about to enter the property. I nod at her and raise my hand in a stop position. She and the team stop and duck down out of sight since we don't know if Kye has any men inside and watching the house. I'm presuming not since I made it here undetected.

Looking back to the deck, my eyes widen. In the few

moments I was watching the street, Kye has pulled out his gun and the barrel is currently pressed into Corey's temple. "Fuck, fuck, fuck," I whisper, just as Baylor begins walking over to them.

"If you love me at all, Kye, you will not pull that trigger." Her voice is strong but I can tell from the shaking of her body, she's shit scared right now.

"What makes you think I still love you?" Kye sneers at her.

Baylor, reaches up and cups his cheek. "I'm Baylor fucking Evans, everyone fucking loves me."

A grin appears on my face, only Baylor could, and would, say that. Kye slides his arm around her and slams his lips to hers. I see the moment Cox's heart breaks. He's fallen hard for her but right now, he feels betrayed by her. Her acting is on point but then again, fear causes people to do crazy things. I hope he knows she's acting. Well, I hope she is, otherwise this situation has just taken another turn I never saw coming.

"Fuck I've missed those lips," Kye croons, and I see Corey's face once again shatter at Baylor's betrayal, but I'm positive she's playing Kye's game. I've lived with the two of them these past few weeks and their connection is strong.

She takes his hand in hers. "Let's get out of here," she tells him, trying to pull him away from Corey and Avery, that slight movement shows me this is all a ruse to save Corey and her sister, who is a blubbering mess.

I miss exactly what Baylor says next but it's enough for Avery to plead with her. "Bay, what are you doing?"

Bay ignores her and tugs on Vlahos's hand again, but he pulls and stops her in her tracks. "Not so fast, Sugar. Before we go, you have a choice to make."

"And what choice might that be?" she sasses.

"Her or him?"

"Excuse me?" she huffs. I don't think she was prepared for this. Seems she has underestimated Kye Vlahos once again.

"In order for us to leave, someone needs to die. You, as my queen, get to choose who lives and who dies."

Dean grabs Ave and marches her over to Corey. He pushes her to her knees and roughly squeezes her shoulder.

Nearby a woman laughs; it's Monica. She walks, well saunters, toward Kye and Baylor. "She can't choose, Kye, because she loves him." She points to Cox. "It's written all over her face. She's never loved you, not like I do. I'm your true queen, Kye. Give me that gun and I will prove how much I'm yours. I'll kill—"

A gunshot rings out and Monica's body falls to the deck in a heap. Everyone is open mouthed and in shock. "No one threatens my queen or tells me what to do." He looks back to Baylor and cups her cheek again. Ignoring the fact he just killed a woman. Sure, she was a bitch but no one deserves to die like that. "Now, who do you choose?"

"I...I..." Baylor is in shock and is mumbling.

"Time's up, bitch," he snarls. "Time to choose who lives...and who dies."

Shocking us all, Baylor whispers, "Me!"

Dropping his hand from her face, he growls. "Sorry, I didn't hear that."

"I. Choose. Me," she confidently says, stepping toward him. Each word uttered with force and emotion. Turning her head, she tells Corey she loves him before repeating the same endearment to her sister.

"You love him?" Kye snarls, grabbing her shoulder roughly and spinning her to face him. His face is etched with anger and betrayal. *Ohh shit, this is going to end badly*, I internally whisper to myself.

Baylor doesn't help the precarious situation when she shouts, "Yes, I love him with every fiber of my being, therefore, to save them, I choose me! I'd rather be dead than spend a day breathing at your side without one of them here. Kye, you don't get to dictate my life anymore. I make my own decisions and I choose me. You were the worst decision I ever made. I give my life for theirs, it's the ultimate sacrifice I can make." I'm so proud of her for stepping up, but at the same time I'm yelling internally at her because she has just pissed off a madman. And that madman has been known to make rash decisions, for example, Monica. Case in point.

"And that is one more shitty decision you've made, Baylor." He raises his pistol and points it directly at her. That's when I signal for Bec and the team to come forward. Pulling my pistol from my jeans, I quietly click off the safety and make my way to the stairs.

Sneaking up them, I raise my weapon just as Kye flicks off the safety on his. Without hesitating, I pull the trigger and hit him right between the eyes. He too got off a shot and Cox falls to the deck. Looking around, I can't see Dean, seems the asshole got away in the commotion, but mark my words, I will get him. His betrayal will not go unpunished if it's the last thing I do.

Looking over, I see Baylor is frozen on the spot, staring at the scene before her. "Baylor," I yell, but she's so lost in her head she doesn't hear me as I begin to untie her sister's hands. As soon as Avery is free, she races over to her sister, but before she can reach her, Baylor collapses and loses consciousness.

The paramedics arrive. Corey and Baylor are rushed to the local airfield to be transported back to Western General. I leave Bec to handle things here and I escort Avery back to the city and her sister.

If we thought this was bad, it only gets worse in the coming days.

CHARLI  2

…five days later

LIFE IS SLOWLY RETURNING TO NORMAL, WELL FOR EVERYONE else it is, but for me, I'm stuck in a rut. I keep focusing on the betrayal of my partner and it's really pissing me off that I'm pissed off. I'm still flabbergasted my partner turned and betrayed me. He was working for the enemy and I never saw it coming. After we apprehended the asshole at the hospital, he remained tight-lipped as to why he did what he did, but one of these days he will give me the answers I deserve. It's the least he can do for betraying me like he did.

The funny thing about the whole situation, I'm not pissed that he turned, what I'm most annoyed about is I didn't see it happening. We were living under the same roof and he was doing it right under my nose. What kind of shitty agent does that make me?

Internal Affairs is taking their sweet-ass time with

their investigation. However, I'm not worried because I know I've done nothing wrong and clearly my boss, Amanda, agrees, because a new partner has been assigned. I hate that everyone in the office now looks at me differently. I'm the sucker who missed her partner joining the dark side. Well, fuck them. Fuck them all. When my new partner arrives next week, I'll be watching them like a hawk, I will not be made a fool of again. Fool me once, shame on you. Fool me twice, shame on me.

Deciding to torture myself a little more, I paid Dean another visit, hoping to get finally answers. But like the dickwad asshole he is, he's refusing to give me anything. *Asshole.* I almost wish we never apprehended him at the hospital, because seeing him and not getting closure is more frustrating than if we'd never arrested him—out of sight, out of mind kind of thing.

After my third visit with him, I'm still no closer to finding out why he did what he did and I won't be able to put it aside until I do. Why did he turn? What made him turn his back on the oath he swore to uphold? Was he forced? Was I just blind to what was in front of me? So many unanswered questions.

"Fucking asshole," I mumble to myself, as I lean back in my chair and think over the meeting just now with him…

…*"Just tell me why?" I plead with him.*

"Why?" He nonchalantly replies, shrugging his shoulders. "You owe me."

"I don't owe you shit, Davis. I did it, I turned. The end."

"But why, Dean? This isn't the Dean I know."

"Clearly, you didn't know me like you thought you did." He looks down and quietly adds, "I had no choice."

"Everyone has a choice, Dean."

His head snaps up, obviously I wasn't meant to hear that. "That's your problem, Davis. You think everything is black-and-white. Life isn't all unicorns and rainbows, the sooner you realize that the sooner you can move on."

"I will never let this go, Dean. I cannot move on until I get answers."

"Well, you will die an information-less old lady."

Standing up, I shake my head at him and turn toward the door. With my hand on the handle, I look over my shoulder at him. "Dean, I'm not going anywhere. I will be back here each and every week, until I get my answers."

"Don't hold your breath because I will never tell."

Stepping out of the room, I close the door and lean against it. Dean is a stubborn asshole but I'm even more stubborn. I will get my answers, I refuse to give up…

A knock on my door has me lifting my head and I see Bec standing there. "You went to see him again, didn't you?"

"Maaaaaybe," I say, drawing out the word.

"You are a glutton for punishment, Charli. He's never going to tell you anything."

"But I need to know why. I need to know how I missed what was happening right under my nose."

"It wasn't just you he fooled, he fooled us all."

"But—"

"Not buts, Charlotte."

"Ohh, you mean business, you real named me. Next thing you'll be middle naming me too."

"If I knew your middle name, I would."

"Thankfully for all involved no one knows my middle name."

"One day I will find out, and then it's on."

"Whatever, Rebecca."

She flips me the bird and walks out of my office and my phone pings with a text from Bay.

BAYLOR: *You + me + wine + cheese*

CHARLI: *Do we have to go out?*

BAYLOR: *Yes, we are going out for girls' night*

BAYLOR: *No arguments*

BAYLOR: *Meet you at Bin 501 at 6 p.m. sharp*

CHARLI: *If you promise to be on time, I can agree to this*

BAYLOR: *…or close to 6*

BAYLOR: *……this is me after all*

CHARLI: *FINE…you, but you are buying the wine and cheese*

BAYLOR: *deal…see you later*

CHARLI: *Bye, you bully*

BAYLOR: *You love me*

CHARLI: *No, I love wine and cheese*

BAYLOR: *with a side of Baylor*

CHARLI: *6pm, don't be late*

Looks like I now have plans this evening. After seeing Dean, I'm not really in the mood but have you ever tried to say no to Baylor Evans? Yeah, no one has. That woman has you agreeing before you have even processed what's happening. She seriously could sell ice to Eskimos…but I wouldn't have her any other way. Life is definitely more fun with Baylor in it and I can say, without her by my side through Dean's betrayal, I'd be a quivering mess in the corner, drinking wine and eating cheese alone. She's become my person since the shit hit the fan, and I'm thankful every day she fell into my life.

With my new plans set, I head home to get ready for a night that will once again change everything.

DOMINIC 3

GETTING TRANSFERRED TO THE CHICAGO OFFICE CAME AT THE perfect time. Things with Bianca ended badly and the relocation was just what my soul needed, plus a good friend of mine recently opened a wine bar here and well, wine. Once I'd signed the transfer papers, I packed up all my shit and shipped it off. Then I jumped on my Ducati and started my cross-country road trip to the Windy City. I was on a time crunch so I couldn't take my time and really enjoy the ride, but being on the road was just what I needed to clear my head and be ready for the new adventure ahead. One day, I'd like to do it again and take my time so I can enjoy in the sights along the way.

I've unpacked the last box and I flop onto my black sofa. I lean back and let the cushions envelop me. This was the reason I bought it, the comfort is next level and recently, it was where I slept most nights. Lifting my feet and resting them on the coffee table, I close my eyes and let out a sigh. I'd love nothing more than to drift off to sleep but I've arranged to meet up with my old school friend, Branson Holmes, at his wine bar tonight. He and his brother, Kody, started it together. He runs it by himself now after his brother was tragically killed. Kody's death was a shock to all and adding to the shock, Branson is now with Kody's ex, Kasey, which isn't surprising really, as those two always had a close bond and most people always presumed he was with her. Guess fate has a funny way of working sometimes.

Jumping up, I head into my bedroom and strip off as I walk through. By time I reach the en suite, I'm stark naked. Stepping into the shower that's large enough to fit a football team in, I turn the hot faucet on and wait for the water to heat up. Once it's steaming hot, I step under the spray. The hot water feels amazing on my muscles, which are aching from all the heavy lifting I did today. You'd think I'd have been stiff after my long ride but nope, lifting a few boxes is what got me.

Once I'm all clean, I hop out, dry off, and change into my black jeans and a black Henley—in case you hadn't guessed already, black is my favorite color. Running my finger through my hair, I style it in that 'I didn't style it, it's naturally like this' way, pull on my boots, and I'm ready to go. Grabbing my wallet and phone, I slide them into my pockets. Then I slip on my black leather jacket, grab my helmet, and head into to the garage. Pressing the buttons, the garage door opens and I smile when I see my bike all shiny and black.

Straddling my baby, I turn her on, and rev the engine. There's no better sound than the roar of a bike in an enclosed space. Once I've had my fun, I drop it into gear and make my way to Bin 501.

Pulling into the parking lot, I kick the stand down,

remove my helmet, and rest it on the seat. Stretching out my sore muscles, I groan at how good the stretch feels and decide that tomorrow I'll hit the gym to get back in shape. I kinda let myself go these last few months. When things started to go pear-shaped with Bianca, I stopped caring. Not wanting to dwell on the past, I grab my helmet and make my way inside.

The door hasn't even closed when I hear my name being yelled out, looking up, I smile when I see Branson walking toward me. "So good to see you," he tells me as he pulls me in for a hug, slapping me on the back.

"Good to see you too, this place is amazing," I say as I look around.

"Yeah, I'm pretty proud of this place too. Just wish Kody was…" He drifts off and doesn't finish that sentence.

I nod. "Sorry to hear about Kody, you guys were always so close."

"Thanks," he tells me, the grief of losing his brother etched on his face. He's clearly still heartbroken about the sudden death of his brother.

Wanting to change the subject, I broach a happier topic. "I hear congratulations are in order," I say, breaking the awkward silence. "You got married and had a kid."

"Yep, I'm a dad now, Kase gave birth to our son KJ and we're currently engaged," he replies with a huge grin. "getting married later this year."

"Well, congrats, man. Seems like all your dreams are coming true." As soon as I say that, I realize how insensitive it was since Kody is no longer here, but before I can apologize, a gorgeous brunette joins us.

"Branson, babe, can you help me in the back please?"

She smiles at me. "Sure, but first, I want you to meet

someone." He pulls her into his side and the look on his face is pure love and adoration. "Dominic, this is Kasey."

"Nice to meet you," she says, offering me her hand.

"You too. And congrats by the way." She looks confused. "The baby and engagement." Her eyes brighten as my words register.

"Thank you. So, how do you two know each other?"

"Dominic, Kody, and I went to high school together." When I say this, a wave of sadness rushes over her when I say Kody's name.

"You and I will have to catch up one night and you can fill me in on all the mischief you guys used to get up to."

"Sorry, that goes against bro code," I tell her, "It's like fight club, what happened at school, stays at school."

We all laugh. "I can see why you guys were friends. I'll leave you to it." She looks to Branson. "I'll be in the office." She winks at him then turns and walks away.

"You did well, man."

"Yeah, I did. I love her with all my heart, but sometimes I feel like an ass because I only got my chance because Kody died."

"He'd want you both to be happy."

"That's true. Would you believe he left us each a letter, basically giving us his blessing? It's like he knew deep down."

"That sounds like him."

"Yeah." He nods and sadly smiles. "He really was the best brother anyone could ask for."

I'm at a loss as to what to say next when, thankfully, he's called away but we agree to catch up later.

Walking over to the bar, I take a seat and wait to be served. Looking around, a feeling of contentment washes over me and for the first time since arriving in Chicago, I feel at home and at peace. Moving here really was the best decision I could have made, both personally and professionally. I'm looking forward to starting in the Chicago office on Monday, and the usual nerves regarding who my new partner is begin to fester. Will we get along? Will we find our groove and be kick-ass at what we do? I really hope I get along with him, or her. There's nothing worse than having animosity between partners, especially in our line of work.

Finally I'm served and I order a glass of red. The server places my glass down and when I look up to thank him, from the corner of my eye I see someone take a seat at the other end of the bar. Looking over to them, my breath hitches in the back of my throat when my gaze lands on the most beautiful woman I have ever seen. Chocolate brown hair. A smoking hot body. Killer rack and even from here, the most mesmerizing hazel eyes. There's a sadness about her but when she smiles, fuck me sideways, she's stunning.

Our eyes keep briefly meeting but she always looks away. Finally they lock on one another and our staring contest continues, but the moment is broken when her friend arrives, snapping her attention away from me. *Game on, Angel,* I think to myself.

Picking up my wine, I watch her over my glass. Her friend takes her glass of wine and proceeds to drink it. They clearly are good friends. She signals the bartender to get his attention, but as he walks toward my Angel, I stop and tell him, "Hey, I'd like to buy the lady there her drink."

He nods at me and goes about serving her.

Once again she keeps looking at me but each and every time, she quickly looks away when our gaze connects. Her friend turns around and immediately spins back to face her. The two of them have an animated and heated conversation. I sit and watch as the bartender delivers my glass of wine to her.

She smiles and nods her head in thanks. Lifting my glass, I salute her and take a sip. With our eyes locked, she too takes a sip. I intently watch as she swallows and my mind turns to her swallowing my cock. I really need to get laid, maybe a night with her is just what I need. I haven't been with anyone since Bianca and after what she did, I don't want a relationship. I just want a night of no-holds-barred fucking and when I see her biting her lip, I know she's the one I want to take home tonight. Lip biting is my weakness and only cements to me, she will be coming home with me.

Bringing my glass to my lips, I watch her and wonder, how I can get her to lower her guard and let me take her home tonight?

CHARLI   4

I'M SITTING IN MY CAR OUTSIDE BIN 501 AND NO SURPRISE, I'm waiting for Baylor. She's late, like I knew she would be. She's probably having wild monkey sex with Corey but if I was blissfully in love like those two are, I'd be getting down and dirty all the time too.

Looking around the parking lot, I realize that the last time I was here, Corey's car blew up after Dean planted a bomb. Then to top off an already shitty evening, Corey was shot protecting me. The thought of what Dean did to Corey, and in general, annoys the ever-loving fuck out of me but tonight is about letting my hair down and having a good night with Baylor…if she ever gets here.

The rumbling of a motorcycle engine garners my attention. Lifting my gaze I see a sleek black Ducati Monster pull into the parking lot. The rider pops the stand and climbs off. Holy fucking hotness, Batman, this guy is at least six foot five and full of muscle, and not in the eww way, in that, I want to lick every crevice and groove kind of sexy muscle way. He's wearing black jeans that accentuate his height and a leather jacket hugs his muscular frame. It's taut across his shoulders and hangs loosely around his ass, his ohh so fine jean-clad ass. He removes his helmet and I let out an audible groan, crap on a cracker this man is stunning.

Like a creeper, I sit in my car and ogle the fine specimen before me. He looks around the parking lot and for a brief moment our gaze connects. I duck down in my seat, not wanting to be caught being the peeping Tom that I am.

Lifting my head up, I sigh in relief when I see that parking lot is empty, except for creeper me.

Grabbing my phone, I check the time and shake my head. "Dammit, Baylor," I say to myself, frustrated that she is really, really late now.

My eyes keep gravitating toward the bike, if I had lady balls, I'd head into the bar and proposition that sexy as sin man, but that's not me. So I stay where I am and hide like the big-ass pansy I am.

After staring at the bike again, I decide to head inside. Maybe I'll see Biker Boy and his fine looks can keep me occupied while I wait. Climbing out of my car, I walk across the parking lot to the bar. Opening the door, I step inside and like a heat-seeking missile, my eyes lock on my sexy Biker Boy and I find him sitting at the bar, alone.

Walking toward the bar, I take a seat at the opposite end, with a clear view of him, and order myself a glass of red and pull out my phone to text Bay.

CHARLI: *Once you've finished getting down and dirty, I'm seated at the bar waiting for girls' night to start.*

Placing my phone on the bar top, I pick up my glass of

wine and take a sip. I close my eyes and enjoy the robust flavors currently dancing on my tongue. When I open my eyes, my gaze connects with him and I freeze. Everything around me fades away; it's just him and me. Our moment is interrupted when Baylor collapses into the seat next to me.

"Sorry, I'm late," she pants, "I was…"

"Giving Cox a kiss goodbye?" She stares at me blankly. "Don't try and deny it, Bay, your lipstick is smudged." She wipes at her mouth and I laugh, "Haha, gotcha."

"Huh?" she asks, grabbing my wine and taking a sip.

"Your lipstick is fine but my assumptions as to why you're late are correct."

"Hardy har har," she sasses back at me and drinks the last of my wine. "That's for being a bitch."

"You love me." I shrug, as I signal the bartender back over. Looking back at Bay, I smile at her but I'm really staring at the man behind her. I can't stop looking at him, he has a magnetic pull that is beyond my control to ignore.

"Lucky for you I do love you. Now, how are you?" she asks, but I'm too focused on him to answer her. She swivels around and I know the moment she sees him because she spins back to me, and her face lights up like a Christmas tree. "You HAVE to go home with him tonight."

"No," I confirm. "I cannot do that."

"Why not?" she questions. "That man is fucking hot. If I didn't have my own hottie, I'd be over there right now."

"Well, we are here for girls' night and he is not a girl."

"Charli," she says, her tone lowering. "Let loose for once in your life. Go and have a night of wild monkey sex with that fine as fuck man and come morning, become straightlaced Agent Charli Davis once again." She pauses and then laughs. "I can totally see why you and Core are friends. You are two straight and narrow peas in a pod."

I process her words and thankfully, the bartender arrives and places a glass of red in front of me. "Courtesy of the man over there." I follow his finger and realize he's pointing at my Biker Boy, well not MY Biker Boy but the Biker Boy I was ogling earlier. I smile and nod my head in thanks. He lifts his glass and salutes me.

"Just do it," Baylor says, and then turns her attention to the bartender. "Can I please get a bottle of that," she points to my glass, "and a charcuterie board for us to share?"

He nods and gets to opening the bottle of wine that Bay just ordered. My eyes keep drifting over to Biker Boy and each time, he's staring at me. Biting my lip, I contemplate what I should do, but my thoughts are interrupted when Bay says, "I'm going to the bathroom and then I'll get us a booth."

Nodding my head, I pick up my wine and take a sip. Just as my glass reaches my lips, a body bumps into me and I spill red wine all over my shirt, thankfully it's red wine red in color and it won't stain, but he spilled my wine and that there is sacrilege. It's the equivalent to a toddler spilling their milk, not good. "You all right?" I inquire.

The guy turns around and his eyes roam over me, I shudder at the lewdness in his gaze. It's nothing like Biker Boy's gaze. Finally his creepy once-over reaches my eyes. "Did it hurt?" he asks me.

"Did what hurt?" My face scrunching up at his weird and random question.

"Did it hurt when you fell from heaven?"

"Seriously? You are using that lame line on me after spilling my drink? The words coming from your mouth should be, 'I'm so sorry, I'll get you another' but no, you have to use the corniest pickup line in the history of pickup lines."

He stares at me and I don't like the intensity in his gaze. "My my, you are feisty. I bet you fuck like a wild animal."

"Excuse me," I shout, just as I feel a heat behind me.

"Yo, dickwad, apologize to the lady now."

"Get fucked, asshole, I was here first."

"Actually, bud, no, you are not number one. This lady here is mine." He places his hand protectively on my shoulder and my body comes alive at his touch. "Now I suggest you apologize and then scurry away before I lose it and my fist becomes acquainted with your face."

Normally I'd be pissed at hearing someone call me 'mine' but coming from him, I want to strip out of my wine-soaked blouse and fuck him like the wild animal Creeper McCreeperson says I am. That reaction shocks me because I don't do that. I don't fall under a man's spell so easily. I'm pushing thirty and I've never had a one-night stand.

"Sorry," Creeper McCreeperson mumbles, his voice wavering in fear at the presence of Biker Boy here. He throws a ten spot on the bar top and walks away but when I say walk, I mean he runs like a scared little boy. Mind you, Biker Boy is pretty intimidating. Whereas Creeper McCreeperson is scared, I'm enthralled with fake rescuing boyfriend.

"Pretty sure he just pissed his pants," I tell Biker Boy. Craning my neck, I look up at him and smile. "Thank you."

"You're welcome."

We stare at one another and just like earlier, everything

around us disappears and it's just the two of us. Our moment is interrupted when Bay returns. "I got us a table." Her eyes widen when she realizes who I'm with. "I'll just take this," she grabs the bottle of wine and her glass, and whispers, "I'll be over there." She turns and walks away. Pausing, she spins around, grabs my hands, and says, "Charli, just do it." She throws a wink at me and then I watch as she walks over to the booth we will be in for the rest of the evening.

"Do what, Charli?" Biker Boy asks me; his voice is deep, gruff and has my body tingling. All that from only three words.

"With Baylor, she could be referring to anything."

He steps closer to me and leans down. I can feel his breath on my neck. Just from his breathing, my body buzzes with anticipation. He whispers, "I think she's referring to you doing me and I agree with your friend, Angel" He stands up and I instantly miss his closeness. "I'll be waiting. The ball's in your court." He winks and walks away from me, returning to his seat from earlier.

Sitting here, my breathing is labored and my clit is pulsating like never before. Grabbing my wine glass, I take a big gulp-like sip, and then stand up and head over to Bay. I feel his eyes on me with each step I take across the room.

My mind is racing with a million and one questions and thoughts right now. Can I do it? Can I have a one-night stand? What if he's a serial killer? Will the charcuterie board have smoked cheese? A random thought I know, but hello, cheese. Then my mind drifts to what it would feel like to have his lips on mine. His hands on my body. His breath on my neck was enough to turn me into a pile of goo and if his breath can do that, then I can only imagine what else he could do to me. Maybe I should just go for it.

Taking my seat across from Bay, I'm aroused at the thought of what might be but also hesitant to take that leap. Looking back over to Biker Boy, I wonder if, just for one night, I should just let go like Bay is suggesting.

Gah, I have no idea what to do.

DOMINIC 5

Seeing that guy hit on her makes me ragey mad. Before I know what I'm doing, I'm stalking over to my girl—yes she's mine, she just doesn't know it yet—and staking my claim. "Actually, bud, no, you are not number one. This lady here is mine. Now I suggest you apologize and then scurry away before I lose it and my fist becomes acquainted with your face."

The asshole scurries away after mumbling a quiet apology. Pulling out the chair next to her, I take a seat. We silently stare intently at one another but I don't notice anything but her. Her friend returns, whispers a few things that I can't quite hear but my ears perk up when she says, "Charli, just do it," before leaving us alone again. I'm pretty sure she's referring to 'doing me' but Charli—beautiful name for a beautiful woman—is hesitant. It's nice to know her friend is on my side, now to get Charli to come over to Team Cruz too. She seems shy so I need to play my cards carefully, but I want her to know how I feel without coming on too strong. I lean into her and breathe her in, she smells divine. Her skin prickles from my breath and I know she feels what I'm feeling too, so I decide to throw caution to the wind and go for it. "I think she's referring to you doing me and I agree with your friend, Angel." I stand up and stare down at her, "I'll be waiting. The ball's in your court."

Walking back to my seat, I have no idea if I have a chance in hell of her coming home with me tonight, but I do know I haven't felt a pull like this in a long time. I don't think I ever felt like this with Bianca.

I can feel her watching me but as I told her, the ball's in her court now.

A hand touches my shoulder and when I turn my head, I deflate when I see it's her friend. She's grinning at me. "Hi, I'm Baylor."

"Dominic," I offer, and really hope she doesn't try to hit on me.

"Charli is my girl and I want to see her happy. I need you to man up and swoop her off her feet, even if just for tonight," she pauses and steps closer to me, "BUT if you hurt her, I will hunt you down and hurt you a million times worse."

This woman is crazy, I should let her know she just threatened a federal agent, but I want what she wants for us so I nod. "Even without your pep talk," I tell her, "I was contemplating doing exactly that but how am I meant to woo her? She seems closed off."

"Leave that to me," she says matter-of-factly and then turns away and walks back to the booth they have snagged. Charli is nowhere to be seen and then I see her, returning from the bathrooms. Her cheeks are flushed, but

I can't wait to see her flushed from arousal while she's riding my cock.

She rejoins her friend and I continue to sit here and watch the two of them, waiting in the wings, or wine bar in this case, for my moment to swoop in and woo her. Finally the moment is here, it's time to make my move. She's giggling and seems to be tipsy. I really hope she's drunk enough to let go, but not too drunk that she'll regret her decision in the light of day when she's sober.

Walking over to them, her eyes lock on me, and she watches as I get closer to her. Her eyes rake over me, and from the glint in her eye I know she wants me. She's ready to let loose and have a night of fun with me as I suggested earlier. "Ladies," I say as I reach them.

"Hey, Biker Boy," Charli says with a smile, her voice deep, husky, and ohh so sexy.

Her cheeks are a gorgeous flush of pink, and I hope it's from my presence and not the wine, then I click that she called me Biker Boy. "How did you know I ride a bike?"

Her eyes widen in shock. "Ummm, ahhhhh, your jacket. It's a bike jacket, not just a sexy leather jacket."

"Nice save," Baylor quietly says, lifting her glass with a cheeky smirk. She takes a sip. "Sooo, what's your intention with my friend?"

"Baylor," Charli scolds, "you can't say shit like that."

Baylor shrugs and focuses on me, raising her eyebrows in that 'tell me now' way.

"Well—"

"A hole in the ground with water in it," Charli says, and then she giggles at her own joke. The sound is music to my ears. It's the first time I've seen her so relaxed since I've been watching her—shit, that makes me sound like a stalker. I smile at her response while Baylor shakes her head and rolls her eyes. "You seriously are a dork, Davis."

"An adorable dork," I add, gazing at her and basking in her tipsy beauty.

"Did you just call me a dork?"

"No, I called you an adorable dork, there's a difference."

"Mmmhmpf." She stares back at me. The air around us thickens. Her breaths have become labored and the pink of her cheeks continues to darken as her eyes roam over me. Then she says five words that make my night, hell my whole year. "Take me home, Biker Boy."

From next to her Baylor squeals and from the megawatt grin on her face, I think she's happy with Charli's decision too, "I'll call Core to come get me." She hops up and walks away to call Core, whoever he is.

Reaching out, I cup her cheek in my palm. An electrical current jolts between us, her eyes widen, she felt it too. "You sure about this, Angel?"

She nods and nuzzles into my palm, "I've never been more sure of anything in my life."

CHARLI 6

I CAN'T BELIEVE I JUST AGREED TO GO HOME WITH HIM. THERE must have been something in the wine, the cheese, or I've entered an alternate universe because I don't do things like this, I don't tell men to 'take me home.' This is so out of character for me but as soon as those words left my mouth, I felt so confident. Now that he's actually 'taking me home' and my brain has kicked into gear, I'm having second thoughts.

His thumb gently runs along my jawbone and he continues to cup my cheek. Lifting my eyes, they lock on his and within seconds, any doubts I had evaporate. Hell, all thoughts leave my brain and I lose myself in his rich chocolate brown orbs. A calmness washes over me and I'm left with a buzzing body filled with desire, want, and need for the man standing before me.

He removes his hand from my cheek and I sigh at the loss.

Baylor rejoins us, grinning at me. "Core will be here in

ten," she says. Picking her glass up, she chugs back the last of her wine before grabbing her things and walking toward the exit. Dominic offers me his hand and helps me out of my chair. Like when he cupped my cheek, a spark jolts through me when my fingers touch his palm.

Once standing, he escorts me outside and we wait with Bay for Corey. I feel bad for ditching her but from the megawatt grin on her face, she doesn't care.

The heat from his hand on my lower back causes my body to react in a way that I haven't felt in a very long time. He's barely even physically touching me and already I want more.

Corey pulls up to the curb, climbs out, and makes a beeline for Baylor. When he reaches her, he dips her back and kisses the life out of her, as if he hasn't seen her for months and not just hours. It's over the top for being in public, but it's them to a T. He brings her upright again and then looks to me and notices Dominic standing at my side.

"Who are you?" he asks, all big brother protective like.

"Dominic Cruz," he says, stepping forward, offering his hand to Corey.

"Corey Cox," he replies, shaking his hand. The alpha male testosterone pinging all around us.

"Settle down, Core. Nic here—"

"Dominic," he interrupts Baylor.

"Sorry, Dominic and Charli here are going to have a lovely night together. She doesn't need you going all caveman big brother on her. Now, take me home and ravage me." She links her fingers with his and pulls him toward the car, as she looks over her shoulder at me. "Don't do anything I wouldn't do," she singsongs as she opens the door and climbs in.

Corey closes it and looks back to us, specifically me. "Charli, call me if you need anything."

Nodding at him, he walks around the hood, climbs in, and we watch them drive away.

"So," he says breaking the silence, "shall we head back to my place?"

Looking over at him, I nod. "As I said before, take me home, Biker Boy."

He laces his fingers with mine and we walk toward the parking lot, his bike comes into view and I smile. Remembering sitting in my car and watching him earlier, I shake my head when I realize all those dirty thoughts I had are about to hopefully come true.

"What are you smiling about, Angel?"

"I saw you pull up earlier and I sat in my car over there." I point to my car. "I was totally checking you out."

"Well," he croons, grabbing my hips and pulling me to him, "As soon as I saw you, I was checking you out too. Seems this was inevitable."

"I don't believe in that bullshit."

"What do you believe in?" he asks me.

"What's right in front of me. What I can see, touch, and feel."

"And what can you see, touch, and feel?"

"You...and I can't wait to touch and feel you in private." My words shock me, I'm not normally so brazen like this. Clearly Bay is rubbing off on me.

"Have at it, baby," he says, stepping back and opening his arms wide.

He stares at me and my body comes alive at the intensity of his gaze. Brazenly, I step to him and I slide my hands under his shirt and up his stomach. My fingers brush over ab after ab, sliding my hands around to his back, I slip them down and squeeze his ass.

"Like what you touch?" he asks me. Biting my lip, I nod. "Well, I definitely like what I see and I'd very much like to see, touch, and lick what's underneath your clothes. Shall we get going so we may touch, see, and feel each other in privacy?" Again, I nod my head. "Good," he replies.

Leaning down, he kisses the tip of my nose. The tip tingling from the connection with him.

He turns around and from a secret compartment, he produces a helmet and hands it to me. "I can bring you here tomorrow to get your car."

"Okay," I say, as I pull the helmet on. I'm suddenly nervous. My hands are shaking and my heart is racing. He reaches out and squeezes my hand in his.

"Let me." Dropping my hands, he reaches up and within two seconds the helmet is fastened and secure on my head.

He throws his leg over the machine and climbs on, never have I seen anything so sexy and all he did was sit on his bike. "Your turn," he says, twisting to face me. He offers me his hand and I take it. Carefully, I hop on behind him. Slipping my arms around his waist, I hold on tight. He smells amazing, sandalwood with a hint of mint. I inhale deeply and sigh.

"Did you just sniff me?" he asks, looking over his shoulder at me.

"No," I defensively return.

"I call bullshit, Angel."

"Shut up and drive," I tell him.

"Hold on."

With pleasure, I think to myself. He starts the bike, the

engine vibrating beneath me. Wrapping my arms tighter around him, I hold on tight. He pulls out of the parking lot and we zip through the streets. The cool wind flying past us but I don't feel it. All I can feel is my body pressed to his.

Even though we are zipping through the streets, I feel safe with him. I have never felt more content in my life.

All too soon, we pull into a driveway and the garage door automatically opens. He pulls the bike in and the door lowers behind us. My heart rate picks up but I don't move. I sit where I am, hugging him tightly.

"You can let go now, Angel."

"Maybe I don't want to."

"Well, if you don't let me go, how can I see, feel, or touch you?"

"Point taken but…" I pause, fear envelops me because I'm don't know how to voice what I want.

He turns his head to look at me and my breath hitches, his eyes are full of hunger but at the same time, they are so calming. "But what?"

"I…ummm, ahh…"

"You ummm, ahh what?"

Deciding to throw caution to the wind—seems to be the trend tonight—I tell him what I want. "I want you to bend me over your bike and fuck me." I've never had the desire to fuck on a bike before, but right now it's all I can think about. This is so not me. I kinda like sexy, brazen, and semi-relaxed Charli, Dominic seems to bring out my inner sexy minx.

"I've never actually done that before but I'd be honored if you'd pop my bike fucking cherry."

Holy shit, he's about to fuck me over his bike.

DOMINIC 7

She wants me to fuck her on my bike? I did NOT see that coming but I can unequivocally say, I'm down with that, so down with the bike fucking plan. This woman looks like an angel sent from heaven, but in reality, she's a seductress sent from hell to tempt men like me…and I cannot wait to sin with her. Not only is she smoking fucking hot but it seems she has a dirty, kinky wild side too. I'll have to thank Branson for inviting me out tonight, "Ohh shit," I mumble.

"What?" she asks, her voice laced with concern and it hits me she possibly thinks I don't want this anymore.

"It's nothing," I reassure her.

"I can go if you like," she offers, her voice quivering.

"That is the last fucking thing I want. You are not going anywhere, Angel, until you are well fucked. The ohh shit was in reference to not saying bye to the owner of Bin 501."

"You know the owner?"

"Yeah, he's why I was there tonight. Wine bars are not usually my thing—"

"Ohh," she quietly says, interrupting me. "That place is my favorite."

"Weeeelll, Angel, it just so happens, it's now a favorite of mine, but I think it's more to do with a sexy as fuck patron than the delicious wines on offer." She smiles at my words and it lights up her face in the dim garage light. "Rumor has it, you would like to be fucked on my bike." She shyly nods and bites her lip. "Since this is your fantasy, how shall we proceed?"

My eyes drop to her teeth digging into her plump bottom lip, my cock twitches at the motion. He's done that several times now when it comes to my Angel. "Fuck, I love when you do that."

"Do what?"

Lifting my hand, I run the pad of my thumb along her lip, "When you bite your lip, makes me want to bite it… and more."

She leans into me and whispers, "I'd like that very much. However, right now, I need you to climb off your bike and remove your clothes, BUT I want you to do it slowly so I can admire your body."

"And what will you do while I strip for you?"

Lifting her hand she waves her fingers in front of my face. I grab her wrist and gently squeeze, "Uhhhh uh, Angel, all your pleasure will come from me tonight…all of it."

"Well, you better get to it, Biker Boy…I'm waiting and I don't like to be kept waiting." She rakes her gaze over me. "I really want to see what's hidden under your clothes."

"You and me both, Angel, but in order for me to do that, I need to reluctantly let go of you. However, I absolutely promise, as soon as I'm as naked as the day I was born you can touch me, again. And again. Anywhere and everywhere, all night long. But first, let's make your bike fucking fantasy a reality."

She swallows deeply and nods. Letting go of her wrist, I climb off without bumping her. Spinning to face her, I grab my shirt at the neck and pull it over my head and drop it to the ground.

"I said slowly," she scolds me.

"My apologies but at the thought of you naked on my bike, I can't go slow."

She smirks at me and nods. "Fair enough." We stare intently at one another. "Well then, have at it, Biker Boy."

With my eyes locked on her, I flip open the button on my jeans and slowly lower the zipper. Gripping the top of my jeans, I pull them and my briefs down. My cock springs free, hitting my stomach. Her eyes bug wide open when she sees my dick. In a very non-sexy manner, I kick off my shoes and clothing, leaving me gloriously naked in front of the sexiest chick to ever sit on my bike.

"I think we have a problem," I tell her.

"What's that?" she huskily replies.

"You have far too many clothes on."

"That's an easy fix." She sits up straight and spins her leg over, now sitting sidesaddle on my bike. She slips her hand under the spaghetti strap of her navy top and slides it down her arm and repeats the process on the other side. Slipping her arms out, she grabs the material at her breasts and pulls it down, baring her tits to me. Her nipples are dusty pink and erect, begging for me to suck on them. She stands up and continues to slide her shirt down, once she reaches her hips, she keeps pushing down, revealing sexy black-and-white boy shorts. Wriggling her hips, the material floats to the floor, leaving her only in her panties.

I'm so confused right now.

"Jumpsuit," she says, but I have no fucking clue what that means, all I know is that she's now standing next to my bike in nothing but her panties and sexy-as-fuck heels.

Stepping to her, I cup her cheek, "Fuck me, you are a vision." Her cheeks darken at my compliment, leaning down, I press my lips to hers for our first kiss. That electrical current once again jolts us, she gasps in shock, and I take the opportunity to slip my tongue into her mouth. She slides her hands around my neck and deepens the kiss and our connection. As first kisses go, this one is pretty amazing.

Sliding my hands down her back, I cup her ass and lift her up, placing her back onto the seat. She spreads her legs and I step between them. Moving away from her lips. I kiss along her jaw, her head drops back, elongating her neck, and giving me unobstructed access to her neck. Kissing and nipping along her skin, I make my way down to her chest.

Cupping her breasts in my hands, I push them together before taking one of her nipples into my mouth, nipping the tip before sucking the nipple into my mouth. "Nic," she moans as I suck harder. Letting the tip pop from my mouth, I kiss across her to her other nipple. I squeeze it between my thumb and forefinger, garnering a hiss from her. My tongue darts out and I circle the nub before gently biting and sucking. Once again, she moans. Gripping my head, she pushes me farther into her.

Lifting my head, I gaze into her eyes. "Time to make your fantasy a reality."

CHARLI 8

HOLY HOTNESS, BATMAN, THIS MAN IS FINE. ALL HE'S DONE IS kiss me and play with my tits and my body is already buzzing with desire, want, need, lust, and everything in-between. I've never been more turned on than I am in this moment. The hunger in his eyes matches mine, when he says, "Time to make your fantasy a reality," I nearly climax on the spot. Biting my lip, I nod my head.

When he slides his hands down my sides, a giggle breaks free. "That tickles," I playfully laugh.

"Sorry," he responds, with a smirk that indicates he totally is not sorry. He grabs the waistband of my boy shorts and begins to pull them down. I lift up and he removes them, dropping them to the garage floor and the pile of already discarded garments. Leaving me naked, except for my shoes on his bike. "Fuuuuck, Angel, you are...I have no words."

"I could say the same about you," I pause and bite my lip, "now fuck me, Biker Boy." My brazen words shock me but at the same time, they don't. Clearly Baylor is rubbing off on me, and right now I really want Dominic to rub himself on me.

"With fucking pleasure," he growls.

He grips his cock and strokes it a few times, as he steps closer to me and rubs the tip up and down my lips. Leaning back, I use my core strength to hold myself up and grip on to his upper arms for added support. He taunts me a few more times and then he thrusts his hips and slams into me.

"Nic," I moan, as he continues to slide in and out of me.

We stare at one another as we fuck on his bike. My hips meeting him thrust for thrust. That tingling feeling begins to develop in my belly. "I'm close," I pant.

"Me too," he growls. His grip on my hips tightens, and he continues to slam into me over and over, faster and faster. My eyes close and I scream out his name as the most intense orgasm of my life detonates. My body stiffens. My skin tingles and the air around us zings with electricity as we each let our release take over us.

We are both panting heavily. Opening my eyes, we stare at one another as we control our breathing. Sweat glistens on our skin as we both come down from our euphoric high.

Without saying a word, he lifts me up. Instinctively, I wrap my arms around his neck and my legs around his waist. His cock is still hard and inside me as he turns and walks toward the door leading inside. How he's still hard after what we just did amazes me. He opens the interior door and walks down the hallway and enters his bedroom. He steps through the room and into the en suite. Reaching into the shower, he turns it on and steps in. The cold spray splashes us and we both hiss.

"Shit, that's cold," he says, but the water begins to heat. He lowers himself down and sits on the shower seat with me straddling him. His gaze is locked on mine. Leaning forward, I press my lips to his. My tongue presses along the seam of his lips and slips into his mouth. Our tongues caress one another and my hips begin to circle. His cock hardens further inside me and before long we are rocking back and forth for round number two.

We both come much quicker this time. Resting my forehead against his, we each calm our breathing. "You are everything I imagined, and more, Charli." His places a quick kiss on my lips. "Now, let's get washed, then we can sleep a little, and then we can go again."

"So cocky," I tease him.

"Not cocky, just stating the facts."

"Ohh really," I say, as I climb off him. My legs feel like jelly but the warmth from the hot water raining down on me is heaven on my muscles and I moan.

"You keep moaning like that, and I'll have to take you again."

"I'm down with that," I tease.

Winking at him, I step back under the spray. Closing my eyes, I drop my head backward and let the water wash over me. I open my eyes, when I feel him standing in front of me. Even with the water obscuring my vision, I can see every gorgeous inch of this man. Lifting my hand, I cup his cheek. "Thank you," I honestly tell him.

"Why are you thanking me?" he asks me.

"For tonight."

"It's only just getting started," he says.

Lowering his head down, he presses his lips to mine

and before I can process what's happening, he lifts me up and presses my back into the tiles. My legs close around him and his cock slides into me again. Our bodies join as one, it's as if we were made from the same mold.

"Nic," I moan against his lips, as orgasm number three begins to build. Startling me, he pulls out of me and lowers me to my feet.

"Turn around," he demands, his tone rough, but it sparks me to life and I spin around. "Hands on the wall." Lifting my arms, I press them to the tiles. "Don't move or I'll stop and we will go to bed." Nodding my head, I spread my legs and push my ass toward him, circling my hips on his rock hard cock. "Didn't I tell you not to move?" he warns.

Turning my head, I look at him over my shoulder and shrug. He slaps my ass, the skin stinging from the connection but before I can scold him, he grabs my hips and slams himself back into me. Pistoning his hips back and forth. From this angle he hits that pleasure spot. "Niiiiiiic-cc," I moan. As my orgasm tears through me, he follows as I'm riding out the pleasure wave.

He slides his hands around my front, cupping my boobs. Turning my head to face him, he presses his lips to mine for a kiss that takes my breath away. He breaks the connection and stares at me. Neither of us utter a word as I spin to face him. With my eyes on his, I grab his shower gel and squeeze some into my palm and I begin to wash him. My hands slide over his body, once he's all clean, I push him back under the spray and watch as the soapy bubbles slide down his torso. A torso that was carved by the gods.

Reaching out, I squeeze some more soap into my hands and I soap myself up. I notice his gaze intently follows my hands as I wash my breasts and stomach. Sliding my hands between my thighs, I shudder when I brush my clit. It's swollen and throbbing. He grips my wrist, "What did I say about your pleasure tonight?"

"I'm washing myself, it's not my fault that you have my body buzzing and when I brushed my clit, it decided to quiver."

He stares intently at me. "Fine, I'll allow it."

"Tough shit if you didn't, Biker Boy."

Pushing him out of the way, I step under the spray and wash the soap off, paying extra attention to my breasts just to taunt him, but it doesn't work. He shakes his head and steps out, and the asshole flicks the faucet to cold, causing me to squeal when the coldness hits my heated skin. Jumping out of the shower, I glower at him as he laughs.

He leans down, giving me a perfect view of his tight, taut ass and grabs out two fluffy towels. He hands one to me and we silently dry off. He throws his to the floor and takes mine, dropping it on top of his. He grabs my hand and pulls me into his room. He pulls back the comforter and climbs in, patting the sheet next to him. "You coming?"

"I just did…three times."

"If you keep staring at me like that, I'll be making it four very soon."

"As much as I'd love that, my vagina needs a rest. Maybe in the morning, if you don't hog the bed and snore, we can make it four."

"I don't snore."

"So you're a bed hog?" I tease, as I climb in next to him.

Pushing him to his back, I snuggle into his side. He wraps his arm around me and I throw my leg over him.

I'm not normally a snuggler, but with Dominic I seem to be doing many things I don't normally do.

"Goodnight, Angel," he whispers, pressing a kiss to my temple.

"Night, Biker Boy," I reply, pressing a kiss to his pectoral.

Sleep comes quickly and I have the best night sleep I've had in a very long time. Probably because I'm exhausted after three amazeballs orgasms, but it could also be because I'm the most relaxed I've been in a very long time.

Dominic Cruz is the prescription I needed and I have a feeling life will be good from here on out...or not.

DOMINIC 9

I'M PLEASANTLY WOKEN THE NEXT MORNING WITH CHARLI'S lips wrapped around my dick. Lifting my head, I look down and see my cock slide in and out of her perfect mouth. Her eyes are locked on me as she blows me. She winks and continues to suck my dick and fondle my balls. Sooner than a grown man should, I come down her throat. Grunting and gripping the sheets in my fists through my release, she sucks and licks every drop from me. My cock pops out of her mouth and she seductively crawls up my body. "Morning, Biker Boy," she murmurs before pressing her lips to mine. *Yep, definitely the best way to wake up.*

Threading my fingers into her hair, I hold her to me, deepening the kiss and our connection. Flipping her to her back, she squeals, and smiles up at me. Her smile hits me right in the chest. "Morning, Angel."

We stare at one another and something passes between us, but as quickly as it appears it's gone. She reaches up and cups my cheek. "Thank you for last night, I guess I better get going."

"Or…" I offer.

"Or what?" she asks, running her thumb along my jaw.

Leaning down, I nibble her neck and whisper, "Well, for starters, I need my breakfast. You've already had yours. After I've had my breakfast, we can have a nap because when we wake, it will be midmorning fuck time." I nip her earlobe. "Which will lead into our lunchtime fuck," I suck on her earlobe, "then I'll feed you…food as you'll need your energy for your afternoon fuck." I kiss that sensitive spot behind her ear. "Only then, will you 'get going' as you put it."

"I think I like that plan," she breathlessly pants, as I continue to kiss down her neck toward her gorgeous tits, taking her nipple into my mouth, and gently sucking.

"Fantastic, now let me have my breakfast."

She likes this plan because she pushes on my head, guiding me down her body. I can smell her arousal and I've barely touched her. She spreads her legs, opening herself up. I breathe her in and moan before I slide my tongue between her folds.

"Biker Boy," she moans, pressing my head into her farther. "Fuuuuuuuuck," she wails, as I bring her closer to the brink. She explodes on my face when I slip the tip of my pinky into her ass. Sliding back up her body, I stare down at her. Her cheeks are flushed, I have never seen a more gorgeous sight. "We will totally be exploring your ass later."

She bites her lip and nods her head.

"Fuck me, you are perfect in every way," I tell her before I slam my lips against hers. The force of my kiss shocks her, her mouth opens, and I slip my tongue inside.

My cock thickening with each sweep of her tongue against mine.

"Fuck me, Biker Boy," she breathlessly whispers against my lips.

Without waiting a beat, I rub the tip of my cock up and down her slit. She tilts her hips and the head edges in slightly. Staring down at her, I thrust forward and push the rest of the way in. Pausing, I hold myself still and let her warmth envelop me and then I begin to rock back and forth. Her forehead rests against mine as I continue the thrust in and out of her. This is more than fucking, it feels like we're making love. That thought should scare me but it doesn't. That thought lingers in the back of my mind as Charli and I continue to thrust back and forth.

She rakes her nails down my back and grips my ass, pulling me into her farther. Our bodies are one as we both rock our hips. The connection between us is palpable. The air pinging with desire and lust. It's filled with moans, groans, and grunts.

My eyes are closed and I give everything I have to her. Her body stills beneath me and she lets out a guttural wail that sets me off. Together we come and I come hard. Harder than I ever have before. Opening my eyes, I stare down at her. She's breathing hard.

Reaching up she cups my cheeks. "Fuck me, Biker Boy, that was—"

"Amazing. Out of this world. The best fuck you've ever had."

"Wasn't what I was going to say, but I totally agree."

Rolling off her, I lie on my back, and she cuddles into my side, just like she did last night, and I have to say, I love having her close to me like this. Normally after a hookup it's uncomfortable but with Charli there's no awkwardness.

Her fingertips gently run across my pecs, my skin coming to life under her touch. I internally laugh, this woman is turning me into a mushy ball but I don't care. After the clusterfuck that was Bianca, it's liberating to be at ease with a partner.

Seems moving to Chicago was not only great for my career but personally too. Charli and I click on all levels. I wasn't expecting to meet anyone last night but I'm glad I met Charli. She is the complete package. Killer body. Wicked sense of humor. Amazing mouth, but most of all, she's honest and real. I know I don't know her well, but she's everything I imagine when I think of who I want Mrs. Cruz to be. Again, that thought doesn't scare me. I don't think it does because she is who I have been waiting for all my life.

Charli's breathing evens out, she's drifted back to sleep. I stare down at her and smile. *I fucking love Chicago,* I think to myself. Gently I place a kiss on her head and close my eyes. My last thought before I drift off to the land of Nod is that this is the beginning of something amazing.

CHARLI 10

I'M LYING IN BED WITH MY EYES CLOSED. MY BLADDER IS singing out for me to get up and relieve myself, but my bed feels amazing and I don't want to get out. A rustling next to me causes my eyes to open wide and that's when I remember, I'm not at my place…and I'm not alone.

Looking to the side, I'm met with a muscular back. My eyes trace the red finger marks I left on his skin last night. They start at his shoulders and go all the way to his ass. His ass has bruises from my fingers. Between my thighs begins to tingle as memories of last night, and earlier, flash before my eyes. Then I remember I need to pee.

Climbing out of bed, I pad over to the en suite bathroom. Sitting on the toilet, I relieve myself. As the tightness in my bladder decreases, my chest and lungs begin to tighten. My breathing begins to speed up and the urge to flee is strong. "I need to get out of here," I whisper to myself. I wipe and stand up, glancing at myself in the mirror. The girl reflecting back looks like me, but she's relaxed and well fucked. And well fucked, I am. Both figuratively and literally.

Last night was amazing, the best night of my life, but I need to get out of here.

Taking a deep breath, I peek back into the bedroom and see that Dominic has rolled to his back. His chest is on display and I get the sudden urge to lick each and every crevice on his delectable body. His cock rests against his stomach and I remember what it felt like in my mouth earlier. If I was brave, I'd crawl back onto the bed and ride him like the stallion he is, but I'm not that brave brazen woman anymore. I'm back to being a big-ass chickenshit who's about to sneak out.

Ever so quietly, I tiptoe across his room and into the living area. I look around for my clothes and then I remember they're in the garage. I open the garage door and like each time you try to be quiet, it sounds like a herd of elephants heffalumping about. I look over my shoulder but I don't hear or see Dominic. I slip into the garage and quickly redress. Once I'm clothed, I grab my phone and I order myself an Uber. Thank fuck for location tracking, as I have no clue as to where I am. Luck is on my side and a car is only a few minutes away.

With my ride on the way, I quietly head back inside. Tiptoeing to the front door, I'm almost free when his voice startles me. "Leaving without saying goodbye?"

Spinning on my heel, I stare at him, and holy crap on a cracker, this man is fine. His hair is messy in that sexy I-just-crawled-out-bed way. A pair of gray—yes gray—sweatpants hang low on his hips, accentuating every rugged ridge on his body. "I…umm, ahh—"

"Sneaking out so there's no awkward goodbye?"

Nodding my head, I smile. "Yeah, pretty much. Look,

Nic, I've never done this before. I don't know the etiquette for the morning after."

"Sneaking out without saying goodbye is not the best way to end what I can unequivocally say was the best night of my life."

Again I find myself grinning. "Yeah, it was pretty amazing."

"So why are you sneaking away then? We could have this all the time. Maybe?"

"Just because we had a great time between the sheets doesn't mean we will connect emotionally too."

"I'd be surprised if we didn't because, Charli, I have never, N-E-V-E-R felt a connection like I do with you."

I did too is what I want to say, but instead I go with, "Nic, please just let me go."

"Give me one good reason why."

He walks toward me. "Because…"

"Because? That's all you've got?"

Looking to the floor, I close my eyes and take a deep breath, lifting my head, I stare at him. "Nic, I'm not looking for anything right now. If fate has other ideas and we meet again, then we know that it was meant to be, but for now I'm gonna go." Stepping to him, I press my lips to his for a quick goodbye kiss, but as with us, it quickly turns heated. He slides his hand around my waist, pulling me to him. His tongue pushes through my lips and into my mouth. Wrapping my arms around his shoulders, we melt together into one perfect goodbye kiss.

Pulling back, I whisper, "I'm sorry." My phone pings, indicating my ride is here. "Goodbye, Nic." Turning toward the exit, I bite my bottom lip, and breathe deeply. He reaches around me and opens the door for me.

"I'll walk you out," he tells me, leaving no room for argument.

We step out onto the porch and I see the sedan idling out front. We silently walk down the pathway, his hand resting on my lower back. My body thrums with desire from his brief touch. A part of me wants to stay but there's also a part that needs to get out of here. As if the moment isn't mortifying enough, a car pulls up behind my Uber. A male and female climb out, followed by two young boys from the back, they are bickering between themselves and oblivious to what's going on around them.

"Boys," the father says, garnering their attention. The six of us awkwardly stare at one another.

"Hi," I shyly say.

"Hello," the father, well I presume he's the father since the three boys all look similar. "Are you the agent here to show us the house?"

"Huh?" I question like a goof. "No, I'm just leaving…"

"Ohh," he says, and then recognition hits that I'm doing the morning-after walk of shame, and his eyes flick between Dominic and me. With a knowing smirk, he turns and walks toward his wife and kids, leaving Nic and I alone.

Nic reaches out and opens the car door for me. "Thank you," I say as I climb in. He closes the door and I look up to see him staring down at me. There's hurt in his eyes and I feel like a bitch that I'm the reason he's hurting. I knew having a one-night stand was a mistake. This is an awful feeling and it's not one I will be repeating. Ever. One-night stands are not for me.

"Fuck," I quietly mumble to myself.

As the car pulls away, our eyes are locked on one another. I stare at him and his house as we drive down the street and turn the corner. Guilt has taken up residence within and I'm close to telling the driver to turn back around when my phone rings from my clutch. The noise startles me and I jump at the sound. Digging in my bag, I retrieve my phone, and smile when I see Bay's name flashing on the screen.

"Morning," I say in greeting.

"More like afternoon, and where the fuck are you?" In the background I hear Corey tell her to watch her mouth.

I laugh at Corey berating her before I answer, "I'm in an Uber on my way to my car."

"Your dirty fucking skank. I'm going to get wine and then I'll meet you at yours."

"Make it tequila."

"This is gonna be good. See you soon, skank." She hangs up before I can reply.

Shaking my head, I drop my phone back into my clutch and lean my head against the window, and I watch the city go by and think about Bay's words. She's right, I am a skank. A gutless skank who walked away from the most perfect man I have ever met and after the best fucking night of my life. Dominic and I clicked on every level. Our bodies melded together as one. He's ruined me when it comes to sex, never will I experience anything like that ever again.

The car stops outside Bin 501. I thank the driver and climb out. Walking over to my car, I unlock it and climb in. My eyes drift over to where Nic parked last night and my heart aches at the thought of never seeing him again. "Stupid stupid, Charli," I berate myself as I start my car and head home.

When I pull up at my place, I see Baylor is already here. "Hey hey, skanky lady." She sings this in tune to

"Foxy Lady" by Jimi Hendrix as I walk up to her. I give her 'the look' and her eyes widen. "What's wrong, puddin?" Now she's channeling her inner Harley Quinn. My mouth opens and closes a few times. I don't know where to begin, the first tear falls and without saying a word, she pulls me in for a hug.

Wrapping my arms around her, I begin to sob. "I had the best night of my life with Biker Boy," I sniffle, "and then I left, saying if it's meant to be it's meant to be, but I think I made a mistake. I should have stayed. I should have gotten his details. I shouldn't have been a skank. I should have been a mature adult."

"Why did you do all of that if it was the best night your life?"

"'Cause I'm a dickwad."

She pulls away and cups my cheek in a motherly way. "Don't cry, Charli. Let's go upstairs and you can spend the afternoon with me and Jose. We can make you forget all about Biker Boy." She lifts the bag with her and jiggles it about. I can hear bottles clinking together. I nod and for the first time since I got home, I smile through my tears.

Bay and I link arms and we head inside and up to my apartment. She and Jose certainly do make me forget all about the sexy bike-riding Adonis...that is until Monday morning when I come face-to-face with him in the most unlikely of locations.

DOMINIC  11

Watching Charli drive away in her Uber just now gutted me. *Man, I'm turning into a chick with all these 'feelings,'* I think to myself, as I watch the car turn the corner at the end of the street. I'm left standing here with my crumpled heart, alone, but movement beside me catches my attention. When I look up, the man, his wife, and sons are still standing here, staring at me.

I smile at them, the man has a knowing looking on his face. His wife has a scowl on hers and the kids; they are none the wiser as to what just transpired. Nodding my head, I smile, and watch as they walk toward the house next door. It was recently sold, I'm guessing they're my new neighbors. *Perfect first meeting*, I think to myself as I head back inside.

Closing the door behind me, I walk toward the kitchen. "I need coffee," I mumble to myself, as I grab my mug and place it under my Keurig.

Leaning against the counter, I wait for the nectar that is coffee to brew. My mind flits over last night and this morning. I woke up to an empty bed, and my heart deflated when I realized I'd been fucked and chucked. I really thought we had a connection, but the conversation just now proves that, once again, when it comes to chicks, I know jack shit. My dick is rock fucking hard right now, it clearly didn't get the memo that I'm alone.

With my coffee in hand, I pad across the living room and step out onto the back deck. The deck was the reason I got this place. It takes up the majority of the backyard but it's perfect. To the left is a sunken hot tub and to the right is a gourmet outdoor kitchen. I treated myself and have ordered an outdoor table and matching lounger that my sister, Elena, helped me pick out. She's another reason coming to Chicago has been great. I never realized how much I missed her. She's currently a first-year med student at Western General. I'm so proud of her, if only Abigail, or Abi as she prefers, was as focused as Elena. Abi, is the baby of the family and in Mom and Dad's eyes, she can do no wrong. She's definitely the wild child of the three of us, but in saying that, I wouldn't change a thing about her.

As if she knew I was thinking about her, my phone pings with a text.

ABI - *What's up Boogerbutt?*

DOMINIC - *Having a coffee on my big deck*

ABI - *I don't want to know about your big deck*

DOMINIC - *Can't wait for you to sit on my big deck*

ABI - ***middle finger emoji***

DOMINIC - *You love me **kiss emoji***

ABI - *Only cause I have to*

ABI - *Can't wait to visit you*

ABI - *Mom says hey*

DOMINIC - *Tell her, her favorite son loves her*

ABI - *You're her only son*

DOMINIC - *Hence her favorite, der.*

DOMINIC - *How are you?*

ABI - *I'm texting you on a Sunday afternoon so clearly I'm bored.*

DOMINIC - *Feel the love. What's up?*

ABI - *You ever feel lost?*

That last message concerns me so I bring up FaceTime and call her.

"You didn't need to call," she says in greeting.

"I know I didn't but I think this conversation will be easier in person rather than via text."

"I'm fine," she confirms, but I can tell from the look on her face she is anything but.

"Abi," I warn, "don't bullshit me. Whenever you, or any woman, says they are fine; they are definitely not fine. What's got you down?" She goes quiet, and then her eyes well with tears. "You're scaring me, Sissy."

"Donovan broke up with me."

"Well, he's clearly a dick and not worthy of your tears."

"But I..." She drifts off and then it clicks.

"Slept with him."

She nods. "He humped and dumped me." She's full-on crying now.

"I know how you feel and—"

"You don't know shit," she sasses, wiping at her tear-stained cheeks.

"I know more than you think, Sis." My mind immediately drifts to Charli, *I know exactly how you feel, Abs, but the difference is, I'm not a seventeen-year-old girl.*

"I thought he loved me, Nic." I growl when she calls me Nic. My name is Dominic but as soon as I think that, I realize that most of the night, Charli called me Nic and I didn't correct her. In fact, I didn't mind her calling me that at all. I normally hate it when people call me Nic. *Another reason we were perfect,* then I hear Abi say, "...I was only a bet." My mind forgets about Charli and I focus on my sister.

"Say that again?" I growl, my big brotherliness kicking in.

"It was all a bet," she cries.

"He bet on you?"

"Yep, he and his friends have a bet on how many girls they can bang before Christmas break."

"What a bunch of dickwads."

"That's nicer than what I said when I found out. Any chance you can arrest the pindicked assholes?"

"As much as I'd love to help you with that, I can't."

"Maybe Elena can get me a severe shits inducing drug. I can give them all a case of the mega shits."

"Just go to pharmacy and do it yourself. No need to incriminate Elena like that, or ruin her career before it's even begun."

"You're so smart."

"You're just realizing this?" I tease. "But I promise, you'll get over it, and then when you least expect it, you'll meet Mr. Right and you'll forget all about the dickwad who broke your hymen and heart."

"Speaking from experience?"

"Well, since I haven't found Mrs. Right and don't have

a hymen, I can't say for sure but look at Mom and Dad. They're blissfully happy and in love."

"It's so gross seeing old people being all lovely-dovey."

A laugh breaks free but I smile because Mom and Dad are VERY affectionate people. I think that's why I'm a sensitive soul at heart. "You'll change your tune one of these days."

"Yeah, but I won't be gross in front of my kids."

"Yeah, you will, you're a Cruz."

"Thanks, Dominic, you really are the best brother."

"I know," I cheekily say. "Now go to CVS and show that dickwad what happens when you mess with a Cruz."

We say our goodbyes and then I head back inside. Placing my mug in the sink, I decide to tackle the rest of the boxes sitting in my office. Connecting my phone to the stereo system, I get to it. A few hours later, my office and spare rooms are all set up. My stomach rumbles and I realize I haven't eaten all day. Not in the mood to cook, I order a pizza.

Grabbing myself a beer, I lean on the kitchen island, take a sip, and think about tomorrow. I'm excited for this new job. I wonder what my new partner will be like. I've been lucky, since becoming an agent, I've mostly worked alone. This will be the first time I'm with someone for a long-term assignment.

There's a knock at the door, I walk down the hallway and swing it open to find my pizza waiting for me. Taking my pepperoni on thin from him, I head back to the kitchen. I grab another beer, jump up onto the counter, and eat my pizza.

When I've eaten more pizza than I should have, I clean up my mess and head to bed. Deciding to get an early night before my first day tomorrow. As soon as I step into my room, my senses are assaulted with her scent mixed with sex. At the thought of her and last night, my cock stirs. Much like it has all day whenever my mind drifted to her. Maybe I need to visit Bin 501 again this weekend and hope I come face-to-face with my Angel again. Little do I know, I'll be coming face-to-face with her much sooner than that.

CHARLI 12

"Ugh, I'm never drinking again," I mumble to myself as I climb out of bed when my alarm blares at stupid o'clock to get ready for work. The sun is not yet up but I always start my day with a run, even when I'm hungover. I didn't get one in yesterday but I think I got my exercise in another way, so I give myself a pass. I'm still sore, but that's no surprise, because Nic fucked me into the middle of next week, no, year. Baylor thinks I'm a 'fucking moron'—her exact words—for running out on him, and not that I'd ever admit it to her, I think I agree. Sneaking out like I did was one of the biggest mistakes I've ever made, but there's no point in dwelling on the past.

With that thought in mind, I change into my running gear and head out. Jogging first thing in the morning reinvigorates the soul and I always have a great day when I start like this. I'm meeting my new partner today, can't say I'm looking forward to that. After the betrayal from Dean, I'm not keen to have a new one.

After hitting five miles, I make my way home to shower and change. I decide to head in early, to get on top of some paperwork. Since it's early, I stop at the coffee shop downstairs and grab myself a salted caramel latte, my new favorite coffee, and a ham and cheese croissant.

When I arrive at the office, I'm the only one here. No surprise since it's not yet 7:00 a.m. The silence is peaceful and it allows me to get in and tackle the mountain of paperwork on my desk.

A knock at my door startles me and when I look up, I see the captain. "Morning, Boss," I tell her.

"Morning. Your new partner is here. Can you meet us in the conference room in five?"

"Can do."

She nods and exits my office. I quickly finish the file I was working on and then I make my way into the conference room. Amanda is facing the door and a man is sitting with his back to me, "Charli, I'd like you to meet your new partner, Dominic Cruz."

My world freezes when my new partner turns around. My mouth drops in shock and my eyes bug wide open. My new partner is *him*. "Hi," I manage to squeak out. Walking into the room, I offer him my hand and he takes it. Just like on the weekend, an electrical current passes between us.

"Nice to meet you, Charli," he says, his tone void of any feelings whatsoever. It's not like the deep, gruff sexy-as-sin voice from Saturday night/Sunday morning.

"You too," I say, playing along with the charade that we don't know each other.

"I was just telling Nic here—"

"It's Dominic," he interrupts.

"Sorry, Dominic, I was updating him about our

upcoming cases and your current predicament with IA. I have reassured him that you're innocent and he has nothing to worry about."

"I'm sorry you're going through this," he says, his voice showing some compassion, not that I think I deserve any compassion from him after running away like a coward yesterday.

"Thanks, I'm sure it will all be over soon. As Amanda would have told you, I have nothing to hide."

"Well, I'll leave you two to get aquatinted." Amanda stands up and walks toward the door. "It's good to have you aboard, Dominic."

We silently stare at one another. I fall into the chair across from him and shake my head.

"Looks like fate had other ideas for us," Dominic says, breaking our silent stare off.

"I think we, umm, ahh, should talk about what happened," I nervously say.

"I think we should too, but not here. Maybe we can get drinks later?"

Nodding, I smile. "I'd like that."

With the awkwardness put aside, we get to it. For the rest of the morning, I show Dominic around the office. Introducing him to those we will be working with, there's not much to catch up on file wise, as I'm in between cases right now, and well, the whole IA/Dean thing. I show him to his office and tell him, I'll be in mine if he needs me.

I head back to my office and close the door behind me. I rest my head back against the wood and close my eyes. Of course my one-night stand is my new partner, that's just my freakin' luck. Walking over to my desk, I grab my phone and text and Bay.

CHARLI - *So, I just met my new partner...*
BAYLOR - *And???*
CHARLI - *You've met him*
BAYLOR - *????*
CHARLI - *Dominic from Saturday night is my new partner*

My phone rings immediately and it's Bay. "No fucking way," she squeals. "Is he just as fucktasticly gorgeous when you're sober?"

Yes. "Umm."

"And when will it be happening again? This is like fate."

"That's what he said too, but I think it's more like karma for being a ho."

"How many times do I need to say it, you are not a ho for having a night and morning of fan-fucking-tabolous sex."

"Well, considering he acted like he didn't know me when Amanda introduced us, I don't think we will be having fan-fucking-tabolous sex again." I pause, "He did agree to have drinks and discuss things."

"Well, that's a good sign, if he didn't care he'd just play dumb and forget it happened. Me thinks you'll be having fan-fucking-tabolous sex again with him."

"You need to get your loved-up head out of the clouds."

"Pffft, whatevs. Make sure you call me after drinks and fan-fucking-tabolous sex."

"There will be no sex with him, but I promise to call after we discuss things."

"I bet my left nut you fuck him again."

"You don't have nuts," I remind her.

"Fine, I bet Core's left nut that you fuck him again."

"I don't want to be thinking of your man's nuts." I pause and think about her words and then I shake my head. "Corey's nuts aside, there will be no more fucking between us."

"You keep telling yourself that, you'll be banging his brains out later this evening. Trust me because the chemistry between you two is too hard to ignore."

"You know nothing, Baylor Evans," I tell her.

"Don't be going all *Game of Thrones* on me, I'm more like the oracle from *Matrix*, I see it all and I see fan-fucking-tabolous sex between you and your sexy agent." Before I can reply, in typical Baylor fashion, she hangs up on me.

Shaking my head, I throw my phone onto my desk and wonder if she's right. Will I be having fan-fucking-tabolous sex with him again? Movement in my doorway garners my attention and when I look up, my eyes widen when I see who's standing in the doorway to my office. "Darren, what are you doing here?" I ask him, staring over at him.

"I'm here to get what's owed," he says, stepping into my office, closing the door behind him.

"Excuse me?" I question, having no clue as to what he's referring to.

"My brother said you didn't know, but after the mess Dean's now in I don't believe a word out of his fucking mouth." He shakes his head. "I should have known he'd fuck it all up."

"What are you taking about?" My confusion is increasing by the second.

"Just give it up and I won't need to take this further."

I stare at him dumbfounded, I have no idea what he's

wanting me to give up. "Darren, I really have no idea what you're talking about."

"Looks like we're doing this the hard way then."

Before I can reply, he opens the door and walks out. Slamming it behind him. "What the hell was that?" I whisper to myself.

It opens again a few seconds later, but it's Bec standing there now. "Was that Darren Chikatilo?"

I nod. "Yep. He's freakin' deluded like his brother."

"What did he want?"

Shaking my head, I recap what just happened and then add, "I have a feeling I'll find out soon."

And soon is sooner that I thought. With what is revealed, I'm screwed...and not in the sexy naked on a motorcycle kind of way. I'm screwed in the 'better get used to the color orange' kind of way.

DOMINIC 13

OF ALL THE PEOPLE IN CHICAGO, MY NEW PARTNER HAD TO BE her. Guess fate wants us to be together after all. Alternatively, fate is just a cruel bitch who is messing with me. You'd think after the shit with Bianca I was due some good luck, but no, that's not the case…or maybe it is? Maybe I shouldn't judge things until after Charli and I chat tonight.

Walking to the break room for more coffee, I think about the morning with Charli. She was the epitome of professional once the shock of me being her new partner wore off. And after spending the morning with her, I think we will make a smashing team. Now I just need to convince her that we can work outside of the office too.

With a coffee in hand, I head back to my office and I go over the office rules with a fine-tooth comb. There's nothing in here forbidding us from having a relationship so tonight when Charli and I meet up, I'm going to broach the subject of an us. I know I haven't known her, well actually, I don't really know her at all, but I know that we could be something. You don't have a connection like we have for just one night, a connection like that is meant forever. I just need to get her on board with the idea of a future with me.

My phone rings and when I glance at the screen, I sigh when I see Bianca's name. Clicking the red decline button, I send the call to voicemail. Two seconds later, it rings again and again; I decline the call. This happens three more times before I angrily answer. "What?" I snarl down the line, my tone leaving no confusion as to my mood.

"Dominic?" she questions.

"You know it's me, you've been calling nonstop for the last five minutes."

"I need to talk to you."

"Well, I don't want to talk to you."

"Please," she begs, "I've already apologized."

"You think two words are going to ease the pain of what you've put me through? Bianca, we are over. Done. Dusted. Kaput."

"But—"

"No buts, lose my number. Don't call me again."

I don't give her a chance to reply, I hang up. Throwing my phone onto my desk, I lean back in my chair and stare up at the ceiling. Memories of that day come crashing back to me like a heart-crushing tsunami…

…The case wrapped up early and I cannot wait to get home. B isn't due home for a few hours, so I can cook us dinner and then we can have a quiet night in. Stopping in at Jewel-Osco, I grab everything needed to cook pastitsio. I use a family recipe that has been handed down to mamá from her mamá and so on. But no one makes pastitsio like γιαγιά. With everything in hand, I

grab a lovely bottle of red to accompany our dinner and head home.

Parking my car, I grab my bag, the groceries, and head up the stairs toward the front door. I can hear a muffled noise from inside and I deflate when I realize that B is home and it will ruin my surprise. Pushing open the front door, it's me who is surprised. In the middle of our living room is my girlfriend, bent over the coffee table and plowing into her from behind is our neighbor, Lawrence. He has her ponytail wrapped around his fist, and the other grips her hip as he pistons his hips back and forth. The two of them are so lost in their desire, they don't notice me. He roars as he comes inside of her and she moans through her release.

Clearing my throat, they both snap their heads toward me. Bianca's eyes widen when she sees me, in a fluster, she lifts herself up and her head connects with Lawrence's nose. A crack sounds through the living room. He jolts back and because his pants are around his ankles, he stumbles backward and trips over the armchair. His ass and balls in the air for all to see.

"Honey, I'm home," I sarcastically say before I turn on my heel and walk out, slamming the door behind me. I stomp down the stairs and head back to my car.

"Dominic," Bianca shouts. Closing my eyes, I take a deep breath and turn around to face her. Tears are streaking down her cheeks. "I'm sorry," she cries.

"Sorry you cheated? Or sorry you got caught?" My question stumps her, she just stares at me. Her mouth opening and closing. "Exactly like I thought."

"I'm sorry," she cries again.

"Sorry doesn't mean shit, Bianca, when his jizz is currently running down your leg." She looks down and presses her thighs together. "How long?" I snarl between clenched teeth.

Her silence pisses me off, shaking my head, I turn to my car *and open the door. Before I climb in, I look over the door at her. "I'll be by to get my things later."*

Climbing into my car, I start the engine and back out of the driveway. I head over to my parents' house. Mamá will cook me my pastitsio and Dad and I will drink copious amounts of red wine until I forget that I ever met Bianca Rowe…

…shaking away that thought, I focus on the positives in my life. My new job. My new house. Charli and our dinner tonight and as I think of her, it hits me. Had it not been for Bianca cheating on me with Lawrence, I never would have moved here and then I never would have met Charli. "Thanks, Bianca," I quietly whisper, seems her cheating on me WAS a good thing after all.

Sitting up, I grab my pen and start filling out the paperwork I need to file with HR. Once it's completed, I drop it off at HR and as I'm returning to my office, there's a commotion down the hall. Looking up, I see a group of agents I don't recognize following Charli into the conference room.

"What's up with that?" I ask Rebecca.

"Higgins and Laelyn from LOTUS are here, they finally have a lead to take down The Flower."

"I thought that was all myth?"

She shakes her head, "Nope, it's one-hundred-percent true."

"All of it?"

"All of it," she matter-of-factly says.

"No shit."

The Flower is a secret organization that LOTUS— Locate and Oust Traitors of the US—has been trying to take down for years, but The Flower is really good at what they do and no one has been able to infiltrate them. This will be a massive win for them if they can do this.

Heading back to my office, I start to familiarize myself with upcoming cases, I feel like I'm being watched and I look up. I smile when I see Charli standing in the doorway to my office. "Hey," I offer in greeting.

"Hey, I, umm, ahh, need to postpone our drinks. I'm going to assist LOTUS with The Flower takedown."

"Need any extra help?"

She shakes her head. "Nah, we've got this. Can we catch up later in the week?"

"Yeah, that's fine."

From down the hallway someone yells, "Let's go, Davis."

"Catch ya later," she says with a wave, turns, and walks away. She quickly spins back. "Nic, I'm really glad you're my new partner." Before I can say anything she walks away, and once again I realize that I don't mind being called Nic. My cock agrees too because he's harder than steel right now, and it's really inappropriate since I'm in the office. Thankfully I'm sitting down at my desk, a rock-hard dick on your first day isn't a good way to say hello to my new colleagues.

Within the five minutes we were chatting, she managed to reset my pissed-off mood after my call with Bianca, and even though our chat has been postponed, I'm happy we will still get to talk, plus it gives me time to formulate my game plan to win Charli over. Leaning back in my chair, I grin. This is definitely fate at work and I cannot wait to see what the bitch has in store for Charli and me.

CHARLI 14

It's finally the weekend and as I sit on my veranda with a glass of wine and a cheese platter, I think over the past week. It sure has been one crazy ride. First my one-night stand turned out to be my new partner. To say I was shocked when I walked into the conference room and saw him would be the understatement of the century, no, millennium. After walking away from him and regretting it, I never thought I'd see him again but fate obviously had other ideas.

It was a few days before he and I actually worked together, as I was helping Tannen, Higgins, and Laelyn with The Flower takedown. That was a major win for LOTUS and the US in general.

It's only been a few days but Nic and I seem to work well together. And I have to admit, in the sober light of day, he's just as fucking gorgeous and our connection, it's still there and just as intense. It's going to be hard—pun intended—working with him day in, and day out.

Next on the crazy week list was the visit from Darren, Dean's brother. His cryptic visit was confusing but then again, he is related to Dean. Speaking of Dean, he refused to see me when I tried to visit him yesterday. I just want answers, it feels like the dickwad is going to take the truth to his grave. I know that's irrational since we are only in our thirties, but I don't think I will ever get the truth or answers I desire when it comes to Dean Chikatilo and his betrayal.

And kicker number three, happened this morning. I was late after getting stuck in the elevator—that's isn't the kicker—when I finally made it to my office, I was met with Amanda and two new assholes from IA. They are still convinced I'm in cahoots with Dean and they interrogated me for over three hours. Three-fucking-hours answering the same questions over and over. My answers have not changed since I was first interviewed, but they are like a dog with a bone and won't let it go. Without Dean confessing, I have no clue how to prove my innocence.

Taking a sip of wine, I let the robustness of the red infuse my soul and all my worries begin to dissipate, that is until my phone pings with a text.

NIC: *Looking forward to tomorrow night*

After the shitshow that was this week, I kept changing the subject and putting him off regarding us discussing last weekend, but today I relented and agreed to head to his house tomorrow afternoon to discuss us. Well not us-us, but what happened last weekend and how we proceed from here.

Baylor thinks I need to just go for it, her exact words were, "You only live once and amazingly good sex is hard to come by." She's right on that last part, amazing sex is hard to come by and sex with Dominic is out of this world amazing. My nether regions tingle each and every time I think about last weekend, that has NEVER happened before. Maybe Bay is right, maybe I need to go for it with him. Just to be sure, I went through the HR rules and regulations and there's nothing in there preventing us from being a couple, it's all up to me, and him, I guess.

With a sigh, I chug back the last of my wine and head inside. Placing the dishes into the dishwasher, I turn it on and head into my bedroom to get ready for bed. Changing into my satin nightie, I climb under the covers, turn off the light, and close my eyes, but sleep doesn't come. Every time I close my eyes, I'm taken back to last weekend when Dominic and I fucked on his bike.

Flicking the light back on, I reach into my top drawer and grab my vibrator. Flicking it on, it buzzes and then stops. I flick the button—not that button—and nothing happens. The batteries are dead. "For fuck's sake," I moan. Throwing the useless appendage to the side, I lay back and slide my hand inside my panties. I'm already soaked, it's embarrassing how wet I am at the memory of last week, but thankfully, no one is here to judge me. Running my finger up and down my folds, I focus on the task at hand. Separating my lips, I rub my clit and moan. That little bundle of joy zings with desire and thrums to its own beat. Sliding my hand farther down, I slip a finger inside, curling it around to hit that magic spot.

My finger is no dick but right now, it's getting the job done.

When I grip my breast and tweak my nipple through my nightie, that's the ignition source I need and I explode around my fingers. My toes clench. My back arches off the bed. My body spasms and I moan in delight as pleasure ricochets throughout me from head to toe.

With a contented sigh, I collapse and relax into my mattress and blissfully drift off to sleep.

Stretching the next morning, my muscles are taut from my self-induced orgasm, my mind drifts to this afternoon and I wonder what will happen. Will Dominic and I see eye to eye on this? But more so, what do I want to happen?

Sure he's hotter than hot. He seems like a nice guy and we get along both inside and outside of the bedroom. Am I open to a relationship with him? I haven't been in a relationship in such a long time. I've been married to my job but maybe it's time I look out for Charli and not Agent Davis. Work is going great guns so it seems like the perfect time to focus on me.

Deciding to leave it up to fate, I crawl out of bed and head into the kitchen. I smile when my eyes land on the full coffeepot—thank you automatic timer. Grabbing my 'Fucking Amazing FBI Agent' mug, I pour myself a cup. Bringing my mug to my lips, I take a sip.

Picking up my phone, I realize I didn't reply to Dominic last night. Shit, I think to myself, I must have mentally replied. I quickly type out a message.

CHARLI: *Sorry, I mentally replied last night. Looking forward to today too. Do you need me to bring anything?*

Immediately I get a reply.

NIC: *Just yourself will be fine*

Smiling at his reply, I finish my coffee and head into

my en suite to prep for this afternoon. I shave, every-where, not that I'm expecting to get laid, but hey, a girl's gotta be prepared. I wash and blow wave my hair. Deciding to go for casual, I slip into my denim jeans that make my ass and legs look amazing and I pair them with a figure-hugging, plain white tank. And finally, my black ballet flats.

Looking up, I realize that time's gotten away from me and if traffic is shit, I'm going to be late. Grabbing my purse and keys, I head down to my car. Climbing into my mini, I drive over to Dominic's place.

Parking on the street, I look up at his house and I take it in. The other morning I didn't have a chance to appreciate the beauty of the architecture before me. It's a classic Chicago bungalow, with a dormered second floor, a large pine tree takes up most of the front yard, and the stairs are adorned with flowerpots. It screams Dominic.

Looking to the house next-door, I see the man from the other morning in the front yard weeding. I smile politely and head up the stairs. Taking a deep inhale, I ring the doorbell. When the door opens, all breath leaves my body as I stare at the man before me. My eyes rake over his body and before any words are said, I realize I could quite easily fall for Agent Cruz.

DOMINIC 15

SWINGING OPEN THE DOOR, MY MOUTH DROPS AND MY EYES shamelessly rake over Charli from head to toe. This woman is the epitome of a sexy siren and she's dressed casually in a simple—sexy as hell—white tank and jeans that look like they're painted on. "You really are an angel."

Her cheeks darken at my compliment and a smile graces her face. "Thank you." Her eyes roam over me and her smile widens. "You're not too bad to look at yourself, Biker Boy." I'm wearing dark denim jeans, a black Henley, and I'm barefoot since I'm home.

"Please, come in," I say, sweeping my arm out and stepping aside so she can pass.

"Thanks." She steps in and as she walks past me, all I can smell is her. My cock likes it and twitches in my pants. Subtly I adjust myself and close the door. I follow her inside and my eyes drop to her ass, and fuck me sideways, it's delectable. The denim molds to her body, accentuating her gorgeous curves. Swallowing deeply, I think about naked grandmas, I didn't invite her here to fuck, I invited her here to talk, BUT if that did happen to occur, I wouldn't be too upset. I am a man after all.

Stopping at the kitchen island, I grab the stereo remote and turn it down, Mumford and Sons are singing about fucking it up and I really hope that I don't fuck this up. Seeing Charli here again is something I never thought would happen, but it seems fate had other ideas.

"Can I get you a drink? Wine? Beer? Water?"

"Wine would be great," she says, looking back over her shoulder and with the sunlight beaming through the back windows, she's glowing. Like the angel I keep referring to her as.

"Take a seat at the island and I'll get it. Red or white?"

"White, please."

Nodding my head, I grab a bottle from the fridge. I go to twist off the cap and groan when I realize it has a cork. Digging in the drawer, I find the corkscrew and open the bottle. Placing it on the counter, I turn and grab the glasses from the overhead cabinet. When I turn back, I notice Charli checking me out. Internally I fist pump because that means she still feels what I feel.

Pouring two glasses, I hand her hers and when our fingers brush a spark zaps through me, and from the look on her face, she felt it too. Walking around the island, I take a seat next to her. Lifting my glass, I look over to her. "A toast."

"What are we toasting to?" she asks and lifts her glass.

"To us and whatever the future holds."

With a smile that lights up her face, she nods. "I like that. To us and whatever the future holds!" She taps her glass gently against mine and brings the glass to her lips. I watch as her lips wrap around the thin edge. She takes a sip, closing her eyes, she quietly moans and savors the crisp flavor before swallowing.

When she opens her eyes, she catches me staring at her. We silently stare at one another. Her tongue darts out and I follow the movement before she bites her bottom lip. "This is awkward but not," she says with a laugh.

"I know, right? I don't want it to be awkward between us," I honestly tell her.

She shakes her head. "Me neither. I…"

"You what, Angel?"

She places her glass down and stands up. She walks into the living room before turning on her heel and walking back toward me. "I've never been more confused in my life." I go to reply but she continues, "I thought leaving was what I wanted, but then when I left I realized it wasn't what I wanted, but I had no way to reach you so I left it to fate. Fate seemed to have a plan because lo and behold, you're my new partner. And this connection between us doesn't seem to be a one-time, fleeting thing." She's still pacing as she gets this all out. She animatedly uses her hands and it's cute to watch. "The connection between us is there. It's strong, really strong, and I've never felt anything like this before. I feel you before I see you. I can predict what you're about to say. I miss you as soon as you leave and when you return, I feel free. Content. Happy. When I'm around you, it's like there's nothing wrong in the world, everything is rainbows and flowers and unicorns. For the first time in forever, I feel alive and that I'm seen. I don't feel invisible with you by my side." She stops and turns to face me.

"You're cute when you ramble," I tell her.

"I don't ramble."

Nodding, I scrunch my face and playfully add, "Yeah

you do, but you want to know something?" She nods. "I agree with your rambling. Every single word of it. And for the record, you could never be invisible, Charli Davis. You are the brightest star shining in the sky, outshining every other one." Standing up, I walk over to her and take her hands in mine, lacing our fingers together. "Charli, I want to see what's between us. I don't for one minute think we were meant to be a one-time thing, and I think fate agrees too."

"Fate's a bitch," she says.

"A bitch who led us to each other so she can't be that much of a bitch."

"Touché." She pauses and we continue to stare at one another. "So, where do we go from here?" I seductively raise my eyebrows at her and she laughs. "As much as I'd love that, Nic. I want to get to know you in here," she pulls her hand from mine and rests it over my heart, "before we get to that again, but believe me when I tell you, I want that so much." She bites her lip. "Last weekend was the best night of my life."

"Mine too and since I've already had a taste, I know the wait will be worth it."

"The Way You Look Tonight" by Frank Sinatra begins to play and I offer her my hand. She smiles and places hers in mine. I spin her around and pull her back into me. She slides one arm around my waist and the other over my shoulder. Resting her head on my chest, we sway to the music. She begins humming along to the music. The songs changes to "You Are So Beautiful" by Joe Cocker, and we continue to sway to the music.

Quietly I whisper, "You really are beautiful, Charli."

She lifts her head from my chest and gazes into my eyes. Lifting her hands, she grips my cheeks in her palms, leans forward, and presses her lips to mine. "Thank you for a wonderful afternoon."

She rests her head back on my chest and we continue to sway to Joe. I press a kiss to her head and close my eyes, photographing this moment. Cataloguing the feelings coursing through me for future reference because I always want to feel like this. It's in this moment I realize I'm falling for Charli Davis.

...five weeks later

It's the weekend and I'm in my kitchen cleaning up the breakfast dishes. Dominic is in the shower, he told me to leave the dishes but my OCD refuses to let them sit. Those filthy little bastards are sitting on the counter waving their dirty jazz hands at me singing, 'I'm dirty and you know it.' I've closed the door on the dishwasher when "Sexy and I Know It" by LMFAO comes on, I laugh as it's super close to what my dirty dishes were singing at me. I turn up the volume and begin to shake my booty around the kitchen. I dance and sing my heart out.

Spinning around, I jump in fright when I see Dominic in the doorway, leaning against the frame. He's staring at me with a grin on his face. "Don't stop dancing around on my account."

Feeling brazen, I spin back around and shake my booty at him. Gripping my sundress, I slide it up and down my thighs as I dance around. Glancing over my shoulder, I notice his eyes are locked on my ass. I take the opportunity to stare at him. He's barefoot. His jeans are torn and only half of the buttons on his shirt are done up, exposing his muscular tanned chest.

Turning around to face him, I shimmy over and wink, before I spin back around and rub my ass against his crotch. Running my hands up his neck and around the back of his head, he rests his hands on my hips and grinds himself into me.

Stepping backward, I shake my ass once again before spinning to face him. My hips still swaying side to side, I step closer and press a kiss to his chest. Kissing down his torso, I reach his buttons. Using my teeth, I begin to pop them open, one by one.

"Most people would use their hands to undo buttons on a shirt," he says, his voice so deep it vibrates through my body.

"I'm no ordinary woman," I reply with a wink.

"You most certainly are not ordinary, Charli. You are fucking extraordinary."

His words hit me right in the chest. Standing up, I grip his cheeks in my palms and slam my lips to his. Wrapping his arms around my waist, he pulls me into him. My breasts push against his bare chest. The kiss is frenzied and frantic. It's downright perfect, leaving me light-headed and wanting more. Breaking the connection, I drop to my knees and tear at the remaining shirt buttons. They fly about the kitchen, pinging on the floor. His shirt falls open and I take the moment to appreciate his gorgeous physique. Abs upon abs that lead down to that delicious 'V' that causes woman to go cray cray.

Licking my lips, I lift my gaze to his. With our eyes

locked on one another, I pop open the button and lower his fly. Sliding my hands in, I push his jeans and briefs down. His cock springs free, and a smile graces my face when I see how hard he is. Lifting my hand, I grip the base and begin to slowly stroke him. Leaning forward I lick the tip, my tongue swirls around his slit as I pump my hand up and down. His precum coating my tongue. I moan as I suck his shaft into my mouth.

With my eyes locked on his, I relax my throat and take him deep into my mouth. "Fuck, Charli," he groans, as I continue to slide his dick farther down with each thrust. Holding on to his thigh for balance, I suck his cock as if it's a melting Popsicle on a hot summer's day. His hips gyrate in sync with me.

His cock twitches.

His body stills.

He groans as the first spurt of hot salty cum sprays into my mouth. I lick and suck every last drop from him. His dick pops out of my mouth and I wipe at the corner of my lip. Seductively slipping my finger into my mouth, I suck.

Dominic drops to his knees, removes my finger from my mouth, grips my cheeks, and kisses me. Much like the one earlier, it's frenzied and heated. With our lips locked, he shuffles us around so I'm straddling him. He pushes my dress up, pulls my panties to the side, and slides his finger up and down my slit. "So wet," he murmurs against my lips. Pressing a finger inside me, I moan into our kiss.

My hips begin to move against his hand, the pressure inside me building. "Please," I whimper against his lips.

He removes his finger, grips his dick which is once again hard. Lifting me to my knees, he lines himself up at my opening and I slide down his shaft. Moaning as his dick enters me. When I'm fully seated on him, I rest my hands on his shoulders and begin to ride him. I slide up and down his shaft, my thrusts becoming faster and faster. He lowers his head and sucks my nipple through my dress. My head drops back and I let the pleasure building envelop me. He bites my nipple and I scream as a powerful orgasm detonates. I ride him like a cowgirl as I come and come and come. I'm still riding my high when I feel him release inside of me.

Resting my forehead against his, I close my eyes and savor the moment. Both of us breathing heavily. Pulling back, I grin. "Well, that took a turn I wasn't expecting."

"You and me both. I was going to suggest a picnic but I think BJs and kitchen sex was a much better idea."

"We can start each and every Sunday this way from now on."

"I like the sound of that."

Dominic's phone rings but neither one of us moves. It stops, only to start ringing again. "You better get that."

"I should but I'm quite content just being here with you."

"I'm content too, but my knees are starting to hurt and there's a perfectly comfy sofa in the living room. How about, you get that," I nod toward his once again ringing phone, "I'll freshen up and we can have a lazy day."

"Can we have tacos for dinner?"

"Deal." Placing a kiss on his nose, I stand up and offer him my hand. He places his in mine and I help him up. We stare at one another, I know it's only been a few weeks but those three words are on the tip of my tongue, I'm just about to say them when his phone rings again.

He steps around me and picks it up. "Hey, Abs," he

says when he answers, and I can hear Abi berating him from where I'm standing and I laugh. Walking past, I head into my bathroom and freshen up. By time I return, he's on the sofa and has a strange look on his face.

"You okay?" I ask, as I sit next to him.

He nods. "Yeah, I'm fine." Much like when a woman says they are fine, I don't believe him.

"You sure?"

"Yeah, I'm sure. How about we order in our Mexican fiesta?"

"That sounds great. I'll see if Bay and Corey want to join us."

"Perfect," he says, but I can tell his mind is elsewhere.

Bay and Corey are busy so it's just us. We order enough food to feed the entire country. After eating my weight in Mexican, Dominic and I head to bed. I fall asleep after a mind-blowing orgasmcap, my new favorite bedtime nightcap.

Just as the sun is rising, I wake up and feel queasy. I think I overdid it on the Coronas last night and as soon as I stand up, my stomach rolls. I race into the bathroom and throw up. Once I start vomiting, I can't stop.

Dominic is a saint and looks after me. He runs the shower for me and I climb in once the water is hot. When I get out, I feel much better. Stepping into my room, I smile when I see my navy blue pantsuit on the bed waiting for me. With a smile on my face, I get dressed and when I step into the kitchen, Dominic hands me a cup of peppermint tea. "Thanks," I say as I wrap my hand around the mug.

Dominic and I head into the office but a few hours later, I start to feel sick again so I head home. I climb into bed and fall asleep straight away. I wake when there's a knocking at my front door. Shuffling through my apartment, I open the door and see Bay.

"Well, you look like shit."

"Hello to you too," I snarkily reply.

"Ohh, I'm sorry. Hello, Charli, you look like shit."

Flipping her the bird, I turn around and collapse onto my sofa. Bay comes in and sits next to me. "You okay?"

"No," I shake my head, "I feel like shit and I can't stop throwing up. I think the Mexican we had yesterday is not agreeing with me."

"Or you're preggers," she teases.

"Hardy har har, Evans."

She shrugs. "Can I get you anything?"

I shake my head. "No, I just need to get this bug to pass and then I'll be fine."

"Okay, well, I'm going to go 'cause I don't want to catch anything. Call Corey if you need anything."

"Why not you?"

"I don't want to catch what you got."

"Feel the love," I tell her.

She stands up and places a kiss on my head. "You know I love you but I don't do vomiting or poop."

"You'll make a great mom one day."

"I know I will."

"You do know that babies poop and vomit…quite a lot from the little that I know."

"And that's where Core comes in."

"You are something, Baylor."

"Something awesome," she confirms. "Laters, lady."

And as quick as she was here, she's gone again.

Picking up my phone, I see a text from Nic.

NIC: *Hope you are feeling better, let me know if you need anything*

I grin as I read his message, he really is a sweetheart.

CHARLI: *Feeling better. Hoping a good night's sleep will help. See you tomorrow*

Placing my phone on my bedside table, I close my eyes and begin to drift off to sleep when her words cause my eyes to open and I sit upright. "Shit," I grumble.

Slipping on my running shoes, I grab my bag and keys and jump into my car. I drive to Walmart and I race to the pharmacy. With a test box in hand, I head home and make a beeline into my bathroom. I open the first box and read the instructions. Pee. Wait two minutes and then I'll know. It all seems pretty simple but trying to pee on a little white stick is much harder than it looks. Finally, I hit the stick and place it on the counter, before I have finished washing my hands, two pinks lines stare back up at me. Ever the optimist, I think maybe it's a false positive, so I open the second test and repeat. As before two pink lines stare back at me.

Not trusting the first two, I race back to Walmart and grab two more boxes, different brands this time. I pee on the extra four and like the first two, they all come up positive.

Sliding to the floor, I lay all six tests on the bathroom mat. I stare down at the six white sticks, all with two pink lines waving their pee-pink jazz hands in my face. "Shit, I'm pregnant," I whisper to myself.

Lifting my knees up, I rest my elbows on my knees, and cover my face with my hands. I've felt off this past week but I thought it was due to stress, or food poisoning, but no, it's because I'm pregnant. My periods have never been regular due to having polycystic ovarian syndrome, or PCOS, so my lack of period since meeting Dominic didn't really register. When I think of him I smile, he will make a great dad. Sure, this is sudden, but we are in a good place, it will all be fine...but ohh am I wrong. The next day at work, the shocks just keep rolling and life will never be the same again.

CHARLI 17

LAST NIGHT I TOSSED AND TURNED ALL NIGHT LONG. BY TIME the sun rises, I'm dressed and ready for work. So I head in early. I still feel queasy but not as bad as yesterday. With a peppermint tea in hand, I head into my office and start looking over the upcoming case files. At 9:00 a.m. I call my doctor and I manage to get an appointment in forty-five minutes. Calling the boss, I tell her I have an appointment and head to the doctor. Like I knew, she officially confirms I'm pregnant. She does a scan and tells me that I'm roughly nine weeks pregnant. Seems Dominic knocked me up on our first night together.

"How can I be nine weeks along and not know it?"

"All women's pregnancies are different. There are no set rules when it comes to babies."

Nodding my head, Dr. Clark continues to do her baby doctor thing. She assures me everything looks good and hands me a printout. "My baby's first picture," I say with eyes full of tears as I stare at the picture in my hands. The baby just looks like a blob, but it's our baby and I cannot wait to tell and show Dominic.

With a billion pamphlets and some prenatal vitamins in hand, I head back to the office with a stop at McDonald's for something to eat. I tell myself that it's almost lunchtime so it's okay, but in reality, I've been thinking about cheeseburgers all morning. I notice a woman enter the elevator behind me and she's pregnant, my eyes drop to her belly and I smile. *That'll be me in a few months' time*, I think to myself.

We both get off on floor seven. I go left and she goes right, when I look up I see Patrick Fitzpatrick—yep, he's a double Patrick—from IA with the Boss Lady. "Good morning, Patrick. Amanda," I say with a smile, nodding at them both, but the animosity radiating from Patrick does nothing to ease my already churning stomach.

"Charli, can you meet with us in interrogation three, please?" He's all official and stick up his ass like, I don't envy the people in IA at all. They get a bad rap but they are only doing their job.

"Sure, I just need to drop off my bag and grab some water." Not waiting for a reply, I head to my office. Patrick follows me and I notice that he's watching my every move. An eerie feeling runs up my spine. With my water in hand, I follow him into interrogation and just as I take my seat, a wave a nausea hits me. Covering my mouth, I take a few deep breaths and manage to keep the vomit at bay.

"You okay, Charli?" Amanda asks when she walks in.

Nodding my head, I smile. "Yeah, the sickness from yesterday is still lingering," I tell her and silently I add, *"And it will for the foreseeable future."*

She nods and takes a seat. I look up and from the look on her face, I know it's not good news. "What's going on?"

"Charli—" she says but Patrick interrupts her, "Agent Davis, you are officially on suspension. We have reason to believe that you were, and still are, working in cahoots with your previous partner, Dean Chikatilo."

"That's bullshit!" I shout and stand up. "You don't honestly believe I would be involved with this?" I stare down at him. "I—"

"It doesn't matter what I believe and I will ask that you contain yourself, Agent Davis."

Turning to Amanda, I plead with my eyes but she shakes her head. "I'm sorry, Charli, my hands are tied with regard to this, this is all IA."

Dejectedly I sigh and fall back into my chair. Patrick continues to talk and tell me what's going to happen from here on, but I don't register a word he's saying. Once I hand over my badge and gun, I exit interrogation and walk in a daze back to my office. In a matter of twelve hours my life has been turned upside down and inside out, and the hits haven't finished coming.

A wave of sickness hits and I race into the restroom. I just make it into a cubicle before I empty my stomach. Ever so thankful that I grabbed a cheeseburger from McDonald's on my way back, otherwise I'd be throwing up nothing. Grabbing some toilet paper, I wipe my mouth and flush. Washing my hands, I look at my reflection and sadly smile at myself. "Nic," I mumble, "I need Nic."

Exiting the bathroom, I take the long way round to his office and as I get closer, I hear raised voices coming from inside his office. The door is slightly ajar and I peek through the gap. My eyes land on him and I notice that he's angry. A woman is sitting with her back to me. "I don't give a flying fuck that you're pregnant, Bianca. I will not be a part of this kid's life. It's all yours. Not my responsibility."

Those words shatter me. Here I am, outside his office door to tell him that I'm pregnant with his baby, and he's telling who I presume is his ex that he doesn't want to be father to her baby. If he doesn't want to be a father to hers, he sure as hell won't want to be a father to mine.

Walking backward slowly, I turn on my heel and race to my office. I need to get out of here so I grab my things. The air is stifling and the need to get out of here intensifies. I need fresh air and I need it now. Amanda is calling my name but I keep walking, ignoring her. Reaching out I punch the elevator button and thankfully it opens immediately. I can't deal with any of this right now, I dive into the metal car and quickly press the close door button.

A voice yells, "Hold the elevator," but I don't want to be near anyone so I repeatedly punch the close button. "Please, please, please," I mumble. The doors finally begin to close and I sigh. "I'm free," I whisper as the car begins its descent to the ground.

Stepping backward, I close my eyes and my stomach lurches. I'm not sure if it's from morning sickness, betrayal of what I just heard, or at the prospect of losing my career. The elevator doors open into the lobby and I race over to a trash can. Resting my palms on the edge, I empty my stomach. I'm heaving when I hear the ding of an elevator. I freeze, hoping it isn't the boss, or *him*, and I'm relieved when I don't see either of them. It's a woman but that relief turns to dread when I see she's pregnant and I immediately know it's her: she's Dominic's other baby momma.

Turning back to the can, I vomit again.

Thankfully she doesn't stop and from the corner of my eye, I watch her waddle through the lobby and outside.

Wiping my mouth on the back of my hand, I follow the path she took and step outside. The cool air hits my face and the tears I've been holding back begin to fall. Pulling out my phone, I dial the one person who I know won't judge me. Before they say anything, I blubber, "Bay, I need you."

DOMINIC 18

A KNOCK ON MY DOOR STARTLES ME. DROPPING MY PEN, I look up and see the last person I expected standing there. "Bianca, what are you doing here?"

"Hi, Dominic," she says. My eyes are locked on her as she walks into my office and sits down across from me. Why the hell is she here?

"What do you want?" My tone is harsh, but I said all I needed before I left.

"I…umm, ahh, I wanted to see you."

"Why?" I question again.

"Lawrence and I are no longer seeing each other."

"And?"

"I'm pregnant," she quietly whispers.

"Congrats," I tell her.

"It's, ummm—"

Shit, fuck no, is my immediate thought. "Is it mine?" I ask, not sure I really want to hear the answer.

She shakes her head. "No, I'm twelve weeks. The last

time you and I had sex was way before that. Lawrence is the father."

Phew, I think to myself. "So why are you here?"

"I want you back, Dominic. I made a mistake with Lawrence, I see that now. I want you, me, and this baby to be a family."

"You expect me to play daddy to his child?"

"It would be our child."

"No, it's his child. And not my problem, Bianca. You have some fucking nerve coming to my workplace and dropping this on me."

"I'm alone and pregnant," she cries.

"I don't give a flying fuck that you're pregnant, Bianca. I will not be a part of this kid's life. It's all yours. Not my responsibility. Go back to where you came from and work this shit out with Lawrence."

"He...he doesn't want me or the baby." She's crying now, a part of me feels bad for her but there's also a part that doesn't give a shit. She did this to herself.

"Look, Bianca. I really am sorry you're in this mess but it's not my problem. You broke us and any future we had when you cheated on me. Now, please leave."

"I thought you were better than this," she snaps.

"Well, I never thought you'd cheat on me with the neighbor. So there's that." We stare at one another across my desk. Leaning back in my chair, I dismiss her, "Good bye and good luck."

Without a word, she nods, stands up, and exits my office. "Fuck," I mumble and rub my forehead as I watch Bianca leave my office. The nerve of that woman to come here and grovel for me to take her back because she's knocked up...and not even with my baby. Lifting my hands, I link my fingers and rest my hands behind my head.

Sighing I shake my head, I need to see Charli.

Looking up, I see it's nearly 1:00 p.m., maybe I can take her out for a late lunch. Pushing back from my desk, I stand up and smile as I walk out of my office only to be met with Amanda, my new boss, calling my name. Turning around, I face her. "Can I speak with you in private, Dominic?"

Nodding my head, I smile. "Yeah, sure." But inside I'm pissed 'cause I need to see Charli. I need a hug from my Angel. A cuddle from her will make this, and me, feel better. Following Amanda, I enter her office and take a seat across from her. "What's up, Boss Lady?"

"You know I hate being called Boss Lady."

"Sorry," I say with a shrug, but she knows I don't mean it. Calling her Boss Lady is a running joke in the office.

"Dominic, all your upcoming cases are being transferred until I can find you a new partner."

I scrunch my eyes in confusion, "Shouldn't Charli be here for this?"

She shakes her head, "Charli is officially suspended, under suspicion of working with her old partner, Dean."

"That's bullshit!" I shout, "Charli is—"

"I know as well as you do that she's innocent but IA sees it differently."

"Where's Charli now?"

"She left."

"What?" I question. "Why didn't she come and see me?"

"She was pretty upset when she left. I know you two are close so I'm happy for you to head out early and make sure she's okay. She's an integral part of this office and I will do everything in my power to get this wrapped up quickly and have her officially back on the team."

"Thanks, and I will do what I can too." I shake my head. "How is this happening? And why? Why Charli?"

"Your guess is as good as mine, but we need to work together as a team to clear her name."

"I'll do anything to help. But first, I need to see if she's okay."

Without waiting for a reply, I stand up and exit the boss's office. I swing via mine and grab my things and head over to her place.

On the drive over, I try calling her but it goes to voicemail. "Angel, it's me. I'm on my way to your place. I just heard the news, I'm so sorry this has happened to you. I'll be there soon." Disconnecting the call, I focus on the road. An accident on the freeway delays me and it takes me nearly two hours to get from the office to her place.

Knocking on her door, I'm met with silence and nothing. "Charli? Angel? It's me. Open up."

Resting my forehead on the wood, I close my eyes and sigh. "Where are you, Angel?" I whisper. Pulling my phone out, I call her and again it goes to voicemail. I dial again and press my ear to her door to see if she's inside but I don't hear anything. Again voicemail picks up. Not giving up, I dial again and this time the call connects. "Angel, where are you?"

"Don't call again," a voice that isn't Charli's growls down the line before hanging up on me.

Confusion mars my face at what just happened. Dialing her again, it goes straight to voicemail without ringing, her phone has been switched off. "What the hell?" I murmur to myself, as I make my way back to my car.

Just as I climb in my phone rings, my heart deflates

when I see it's my sister, Elena, calling and not my girl, Charli. "Hey, Sis," I dejectedly say on a sigh.

"Hey, Boogerbutt. Why do you sound like your cat died?"

"Rough day," I tell her.

"Wanna tell Dr. Cruz all about it?"

"I thought you were going into pediatrics and not psych?"

"Potato. Vodka," she nonchalantly replies. "But seriously, what's up?"

"Bianca for one."

That name causes her to groan. "What's your witch of an ex want now?"

"She's pregnant—"

"Did you not wrap it with her? Seriously, Dominic, how could you be so stupid? Especially with an evil hobag skank like her."

"Thanks for the vote of confidence, Sis. And for the record, it's not mine. It Lawrence's but when she told him, he dumped her."

"Karma is awesome in this instance. So why, and how do you know?"

"She wants me back."

"Of course she does. I hope you told her to stick it where the sun don't shine."

"Not in as many words but yes, I told her it's not my problem."

"Okay, well that's shit, but I know that isn't what's got you down. My sister senses are on high alert, wanna meet for an early dinner? I don't have to be at the hospital 'til tomorrow morning."

"Sure," I tell her. Even though I want to see Charli, hanging with my sister will be fun. Charli clearly needs time to process this IA thing. Since someone hung up earlier, I know she's not alone, but I have to say, it hurts she didn't come to me. I'm her boyfriend, surely she'd want comfort from me. I know if I were in her shoes I'd want her by my side, but she is in shock and hurt right now so she's probably not thinking clearly. I'll spend tonight with Elena and then tomorrow, I'll find my Angel and together, we can come up with a plan to fix this mess. "Meet you at my place?" I offer.

"It's a plan, taco-man."

Then together we say, "Mexican."

"You do the beer. I'll do the food. And, Boogerbutt, don't let that mole get you down."

"Thanks, Sis. See you soon."

Hanging up from Elena, I smile. A night with her is just what I need, but I'd much prefer to be with Charli. I'll give her tonight but tomorrow, she will be talking to me. Before I leave her place, I send her a quick text.

NIC: *Just letting you know I'm thinking of you.*
NIC: *See you tomorrow*
NIC: *Love you*

Placing my phone in the center console, I drive to the liquor store and grab a six pack of Corona since Elena and I are having Mexican. With beer in hand, I head home and when I arrive, Elena is already waiting for me.

"Did you speed?" I ask her, as she walks into my garage to meet me.

"No, did you go to Mexico to get the beer? My tacos better not be soggy now."

"Suck it up, Buttercup," I tell her.

She sticks her tongue out at me and heads inside. We

make our way into the kitchen. Our brother-sister bond sparks and in sync we serve up our dinner. I place the beers in the fridge and grab the plates and cutlery while she unpacks the food and plates it up.

"That smells amazing," I tell her, as I uncap two beers and slide one over to her.

"Only the best for my Boogerbutt." She raises her bottle toward me, we clink, and I take a sip.

Elena and I spend the night together and it was great to chill and catch up. After she leaves, I grab a shower and climb into bed. I try Charli again but it goes straight to voicemail. I don't like this silence. Tomorrow is another day and this time, I won't back down 'til I see my girl.

CHARLI 19

STANDING ON THE SIDEWALK, TEARS STEAK DOWN MY FACE while I wait for Bay. She pulls up to the curb and I climb in. Without saying a word, she leans over and hugs me, which causes more tears to flow.

She breaks away and sadly smiles at me. She reaches up and cups my cheek in that loving way; it eases my hurt ever so slightly. "We'll talk when we get home." Nodding, she puts the car into gear and pulls back into traffic, taking me to her and Corey's place.

We walk inside and I head straight to her sofa. She joins me a few minutes later with a bottle of wine and two glasses. She pours me one and hands it to me. I take it and I'm about to take a sip when I remember I'm pregnant. "Can I just have water, please?"

"Are you sick? You never turn down wine."

"I'm, ummm, ahh—"

"Holy shit, you're preggers?"

Nodding my head, I begin to cry. "Ohh, babe," she

says, taking a seat next to me she pulls me into a sideways hug. "What did Daddy Dom say?"

At the mention of Nic, I cry harder. "He doesn't want a baby."

"What?" Baylor screeches.

"I went to tell him and I heard him telling a woman that he doesn't care she's pregnant and he doesn't want to have to do anything."

"That fucking dick monkey. I'm going to kick his ass. Did he tell you this too when you told him?"

I shake my head. "I didn't tell him. I just got out of there." We silently sit here and I process my words. "That's not the only shitty thing to happen."

"What more shit could there possibly be?"

"IA suspended me today. They have evidence against me relating to Dean."

"They need an ass kicking too. Fucking dickheads."

"Watch your mouth, Kitten," Corey says, walking into the room. He places his messenger bag by the side table and walks over to kiss Bay on the head. Seeing them so lovey together hurts. He looks to me and sadly smiles.

"How you doing?"

"I've had better days," I tell him.

"IA will come to their senses and see that you're innocent."

"That's the least of my worries," I tell him, and he looks quizzically at me. "I'm pregnant."

My eyes widen when I realize something. "Oh My God, Bay, I ate gooey cheese. I drank wine. I went for a run, I'm bad mom and the baby isn't even here yet. Bay," I cry. "I had sex on a motorcycle." A tear breaks free and I wail, "I'm a shitty whore mom." She wraps her arms around me and the tears continue to flow as I let all my grief out.

"You are not a whore, nor are you going to be a shitty mom. This baby is lucky to have you as their mom and they are even luckier because Aunty Bay and Uncle Corey are going to spoil them rotten."

My eyes well with tears at her words, damn pregnancy hormones. I never cry, but for the last few days it feels like that's all I've done. According to the books, this will be the new norm until my lil' munchkin arrives.

The three of us eat dinner that Corey cooked and I have thirds, it's was yummy, and I wash it all down with two bowls of ice cream. The ice cream is not because of the pregnancy; it's my go-to food when I'm upset. And with the upsetting events from today, I deserve ALL the ice cream.

Saying good night to Bay and Corey, I head toward the spare room. Changing into a nightshirt that Bay gave me, I crawl into bed and take a deep breath as I turn my phone back on. It goes ballistic in my hand. I have a gazillion missed calls, voicemails, and texts. I click on Dominic's texts and read over them.

The last one, I keep reading over and over.

NIC: *Love you*

He loves me but he won't love you, I think to myself, rubbing my still flat belly. I alternate between reading his texts and staring at the ceiling. This time when I read his text, anger builds within me. I'm just about to place my phone down when it pings in my hand and I see his name on the screen.

NIC: *Good night, Angel. Please let me know you're okay? We will get through this IA thing. I promise.*

A laugh escapes me, I completely forgot about that. I've been so focused on being pregnant and alone that I forgot my job is in jeopardy right now. Seems my life is just one big shitshow right now. And then he follows up with another text.

NIC: *Just remember, I love you*

"You love me but you won't love our baby," I whisper to myself, as another avalanche of tears break free. Stupid pregnancy hormones. I choke on a sob and let out a guttural cry.

The door to my room opens and Bay walks over to the bed, climbs in, and pulls me into her arms. She hugs me tightly and whispers, "Shhhh," over and over as I continue to cry.

"What am I going to do?" I blubber into her shoulder.

"Be the super awesome kick-ass person that you are. We'll clear your name and then you can focus on being the best mom to BJ."

"BJ?" I question.

"Baylor Junior."

For the first time all day, I laugh. It turns into a full-on belly laugh as I think about the name she suggested. "I am NOT calling my baby BJ. I'll save that name for your and Core's baby."

"Ohh, yes, good call. BJ is mine."

"Do I want to know why you two are discussing BJs right now?" Corey asks, leaning against the doorframe.

"See?" I tell Bay, "People immediately go to a blow job and not Baylor Junior."

"You're going to call the baby Baylor Junior?" Corey asks.

"No," I say while Bay says, "We are."

"We're pregnant?" he asks her.

"Not yet, but when we are we will call our lil' girl BJ and if it's a boy, CJ."

"I like that," he says.

Hearing him so excited for their nonexistent children hurts and I begin to cry again. "Why can't Nic be like Core is over your fictional babies?" I hiccup on a sob. "I'm going to be alone, fat, and pregnant in jail."

"You won't be in jail," Bay tells me. "I'm going to prove your innocence."

"How?"

"I haven't figured that out yet, but I promise you, your lil' Jelly Bean will NOT be born in jail and you will not be alone. Babe, I'll be by your side every step of the way."

"What did I do to deserve you?"

"Swore to protect me when my life spiraled out of control 'cause of the dumb decisions I made when I was a whorebag." She pauses. "You know, that right there is why you will be the best mom in the entire universe. Charli, you have a heart of gold. You're kick-ass. You're strong and resilient AAAAAND you're going to be the hottest pregnant woman ever…well, until I get pregnant that is."

A smile graces my face. "Thank you. You always know how to cheer me up."

"I know," she cheekily says. On anyone else it would sound cocky but coming from Baylor, it's not. That's just her. "Now, get some sleep, tomorrow we figure out how to get you out of the shit mess you are in."

"You don't have to do that."

"Yeah, I do, 'cause if it wasn't for me, Dean wouldn't have gotten involved with Kye and you wouldn't be in this mess."

"This isn't your fault."

"Not directly it isn't, but because of me and my shitty decisions, you are now in this mess. I refuse to let you wear orange 'cause it really doesn't go with your complexion."

"You really are something else, Baylor Evans soon-to-be Cox."

And with that, she and Corey leave me alone with my thoughts. My mind drifts to Nic. "Why couldn't you be happy for this?" I whisper to the room, sadly adding, "Guess I didn't know you as well as I thought."

DOMINIC 20

IT'S LUNCHTIME AND I STILL HAVEN'T SEEN OR HEARD FROM Charli. It's not like her to go off the grid like this. Then again, I've never been suspended from the job that I love, and Charli loves her job with all her heart and soul. Heading to the break room, I see Corey is making a coffee. "Hey," I say as I grab my mug.

He head nods and quickly exits the break room. *That was weird*, I think to myself as I make my own coffee. With my mug in hand, I head toward his office. I knock on the door, he looks up and there's a murderous look on his face. "Cruz," he says, his tone anything but friendly.

"Got a minute."

"Nope." His curt one word answer confuses me even more.

"When you have time, I'd love to bounce ideas off you."

"Mmmhmpf," he nonchalantly replies. The air is stifling. Animosity is radiating off him in droves. He looks up at me and shakes his head. "You have some nerve coming in here acting like nothing is wrong."

"Huh?"

"Stop playing dumb and get out of my sight."

His dismissal is confusing but not wanting to enrage him further, I leave him alone. Guess he won't be helping me to come up with a plan to clear Charli's name. Heading back to my office, I grab my phone and dial her number, again. This time it rings and my heart beats faster at the thought of hearing her voice. And I do, via her voicemail, again. "Charli, Angel, it's me, again. Please call me. I'm worried about you."

Throwing my phone on my desk, I lean back in my chair and sigh. "Where are you, Charli?" I mumble when there's a knock at my door. "Hey, Bec, what's up?"

"How are we going to clear our girl's name?"

A smile graces my face and I laugh. "I just stopped by Cox's office to ask the same thing, but he's in a mood."

"You would be too if you were engaged to Baylor."

"What's wrong with Baylor? She's Charli's BFF, right?"

"Bay has the nickname of 'Bitchy Baylor' and she lives up to that name one million percent."

"Surely she isn't that bad?"

She shrugs. "Enough about Bitchy Baylor, how are we going to clear Charli?"

"I have no clue. Have you spoken to her?"

"She texted to say she was fine but we all know when a woman says fine, they are anything but."

"She isn't talking to me."

"Ohh no, trouble in paradise?" I shrug my shoulders. "Well, I can only imagine what she's going through right now and because of her issue, you have been taken off all your cases. She probably feels bad that you too are caught up in this."

"I never thought of that but it makes sense…even if it is far from how I feel."

"Just be there for her. That's all you can do."

Nodding, I agree but there's also a niggling in my stomach that it's more. But to show her that I do care, I'm going to clear her name, and as Bec and I agreed, we need to go to the source of all this shit, Dean Chikatilo.

An hour later, Bec and I are in an interview room waiting for Dean. "What this guy like?" I ask Bec.

"An asshole through and through. Most of his partners would last one case, if that. Charli was the only one who could work with him. They'd been partners for almost a year before the Vlahos case."

"So that's why IA are riding her."

"Yeah, but I know Charli, she wouldn't do what they're accusing. Even his brother, Darren, thinks she's involved."

"How so?" I question.

"He paid her a visit a while back—" Before she can finish, the door opens and in walks Dean. The guard uncuffs him and he takes a seat across from us. He eyes us with disdain.

"Barber," he says, "this is a pleasant surprise." He looks to me, "And you are?"

"Dominic Cruz."

He nods his head. "The new partner…and more, from what I've heard."

"Cut the shit, Dean," Bec interrupts him. "Why won't you tell IA that Charli isn't working with you?"

"Who says she isn't?" I grind my molars at the audacity of this asshole.

"You and I both know that Charli would never do what

she's accused of. Are you seriously going to let your ego bring down one of the best agents we have? She was your friend, for fuck's sake." He shrugs. "I hope you drop the soap and become someone's bitch. You're a disgrace." She pushes back from the table and storms out of the room, slamming the door behind her.

"I think I pissed her off," he jokes.

Slamming my palms on the table, I lean forward. "I will prove Charli's innocence with or without your help." Standing up, I walk to the door. With my hand on the handle, I look over my shoulder. "And tell your brother to stay away from Charli."

"Darren visited Charli?" He seems genuinely shocked by this.

"Don't play dumb, you know he visited her. How about you give him what he wants and clear Charli's name at the same time."

"You don't know what you're talking about. Tell that bitch to watch her back." That line pisses me off, I turn around and without thinking, I walk over to him and slam my fist into his face. His nose crunches under the force, with a satisfied smirk on my face, I walk out of the room and join Bec.

"Get anything out of him?"

"Nope, but I think I broke his nose."

She grins. "Well, that's a start."

"He threatened Charli."

"We need to get this sorted and fast," she says. "I don't have a good feeling about any of this."

"You and me both, Bec."

Bec and I head back and as soon as we step into the office, Amanda is waiting for us with a look on her face that tells me I'm in trouble. "Care to explain, Cruz, why Dean Chikatilo is in the infirmary with a broken nose?"

"He fell into my fist." She eyes me. "He threatened Charli, I couldn't let him get away with that."

"As much as I admire you standing up for your partner, you can't go around assaulting people." She pauses. "Next time, get him in the ribs, that's easier to blame on a table."

"Yes, Boss."

"Good. Now, did you get anything from him?"

"Nope," I say, shaking my head. "He seemed shocked that Darren paid Charli a visit. This whole thing doesn't make sense. Both Dean and Charli's financials are clean. What was Dean doing for Vlahos? And what does Darren think Charli has? There are too many pieces and none of them fit together."

"Hope you like puzzles," she tells me.

"Not so much, but I will give this puzzle my all. If only to clear Charli's name."

"Speaking of, how is she?"

"I don't know. She won't talk to me."

"She's fine." Cox says, and I swear I hear him silently add, "not that you deserve to know." He walks toward the elevator with his messenger bag on his shoulder, not offering any further information.

"Give her time, this must me hard on her," Amanda tells me, as she squeezes my shoulder and makes her way back to her office. Grabbing my phone, I dial Charli again. And again, it rings out. It doesn't even go to voicemail this time. I'm starting to get worried but what can I do?

CHARLI 21

It's been three days since shit hit the fan. I'm still hiding out at Bay and Corey's place. Dominic is relentless with trying to reach me, but I keep playing what I heard over and over in my mind.

"I don't give a flying fuck that you're pregnant. I will not be a part of this kid's life. It's all yours. Not my responsibility."

How could I have been so wrong about him? I never thought he would be so heartless. I guess it's good that I knew before I told him, if he'd said that to my face I would have been more gutted than I am right now. Sitting on the floor in Bay's guest bathroom, I lean back against the tub after vomiting, again. Closing my eyes, I take deep a breath and find the sickness disappearing…probably 'cause there's nothing left in my body to throw up.

"Stronger" by Britney Spears starts playing from the living room and as I sit here and listen to the words, they hit me hard. I am strong and I will be fine. I don't need *him* by my side to raise munchkin because I'm kick-ass and strong, just like lil' munchkin who's growing in my stomach.

Standing up, I rinse my mouth and then stare at my reflection. I may look like shit right night—thanks, morning sickness—but I'm tough. I will get through this. I'll put my big girl panties on and tell Nic that he's going to be a father. I would never hide something like that from him but before I tell him, I need to look after me. A few more days won't hurt, I'm just not there mentally yet, but I will get there because I'm Charli fucking Davis, kick-ass agent…and soon-to-be mom. I need to be strong for this baby since I will be all he or she has. At least I have Momma and Daddy on my team. That conversation went much better than I thought it would have…

…My head is in the toilet again, whoever dubbed it morning sickness is a lying asshole. It hits at any time of the day and can last for a few minutes or a few hours. I was worried with how much I was throwing up, but Dr. Clark assures me that it's normal to which I replied, "Well, normal sucks."

My phone rings and I reach up to grab it off the counter. I smile when I see it's Mom. "Hey, Momma," I say as I answer.

"How's my baby girl?" Hearing her cheery voice sets me off and I begin to cry.

"It's all turned to poo, Momma."

"Frank, get in here," she yells, "Charli Bear needs us."

"I'm fine, Momma."

"We all know what fine means."

This causes me to laugh. "Daddy is here, we are switching to FaceTime." It rings and I answer the call.

"Ohh, baby, what's wrong?"

"Everything," I cry. Momma and Daddy let me cry, they

offer sweet nothings but I don't hear them because I'm too busy crying like a baby.

"Charli Bear," Daddy says, "what's going on?"

"I'm suspended and…and…I'm pregnant."

"We're gonna be grandparents?" Momma asks.

"Yes, but he doesn't want me, or the baby."

"Say that again, Charli Bear? Because I'm sure I heard that he has abandoned you."

"I overheard Nic telling a woman who's also pregnant that it's not his problem."

"Who was this woman? How many women has he knocked up? I'm not sure I want him to be a part of yours or this baby's life."

"I don't know, I ran away."

"Charli," Mom says in the mom tone, "does he know?" I shake my head. "Charli, you need to tell him. Maybe it will be different with you."

"But what if he doesn't want me? I don't think I can do this on my own."

"You won't be alone. Daddy and I will be there for you, you know that."

"I know but my life is in the toilet right now, much like my head."

"Is the morning sickness bad?"

"Bad is an understatement."

"When Mom was pregnant with you, she too had horrible sickness at any time of the day. She also ate Brussels sprouts by the ton."

"No wonder I hate those green slimly suckers."

We all laugh.

"Now, what's this suspension all about?" Daddy asks.

"It's to do with the Dean fiasco from our last case."

"Maybe I need to pay this Dean guy a visit. No one messes

with my Charli Bear and while I'm there, I can kick baby daddy's ass too."

"Or you could just come and visit me and hug me."

"Or we can do that." He looks to Momma. "What do you say, June, we go to the big city and visit our baby girl?"

"Big city? You guys live outside of Houston, that's a big city too."

"We live outside the city, therefore not IN the city," Daddy says.

"Potato. Vodka," I tell them.

"Ohh, I just read that book," Momma says. "That Alley girl really knows how to write dirty and I cannot wait to read the Dirty one, I really hope Maddey ends up with the brother but then again, the SEAL man is pretty swoony too."

"You've always had a thing for a man in uniform," Daddy says.

"Ahh, hello, your daughter is still on the line."

"Down, Frank," Momma says.

"Uggh, shoot me now," I groan but I also tear up. I thought Nic and I had a love like Momma and Daddy, but clearly I was wrong.

"Frank, book the tickets, our baby needs us."

"Thanks, Momma," I blubber.

"You never need to thank me. I will always be there for you, baby. Always."

...Momma and Daddy will be here next week and I'm excited for their visit. I could really do with a Momma hug right now. Don't get me wrong, Bay hugs are good but they're nothing like a Momma hug. If I'm half the momma that my momma is, then this baby is going to be fine.

Walking out of my room, I find Bay in the living room.

Stuffing her face with purple taffy. "Morning, sexy momma."

"Morning," I say, taking a seat next to her. I reach over and grab a taffy. She slaps my hand.

"Mine," she growls, Bay is very protective of her taffy.

"Did you just beat up a pregnant lady?"

"Yep, and I'll do it again if she tries to steal my taffy."

"I'm hungry," I tell her, as I pop the candy I just stole into my mouth.

"Let's go out for brunch then. You've wallowed enough. It's time to get back into the real world."

"Can I borrow some clothes?"

"Nope, you are going to go home to get your own, and I also think it's time for you to get back on the horse, as they say."

Looking over at her, I scrunch my face up but I know she's right. I can't hide out here forever. "Fine," I relent.

"Like you had a choice. Let me go change and then we can go."

Twenty minutes later, she's in a black maxi dress and purple sandals. We climb into her mini and head over to my place. Bay takes a seat in my living room and I head into my bedroom to change. Ten minutes later I emerge in a navy shift dress and my ballet flats.

Bay looks up and smiles. "That's a nice dress."

"Thanks, it has pockets." I tell her, as slip my hands into said pockets, stretching my fingers to indicate them.

"I've always wanted a dress with pockets."

"Maybe we can go shopping and find you a pocket dress and me some maternity clothes after brunch?"

"You had me at shopping, let's go," she says, as we link arms and exit my apartment.

We head back down to her car and as we pull away, I

see Dominic pull up on his bike. My breath hitches when I see him. He looks so freakin' hot on that bike, but then I remember the words I overheard and any hotness evaporates.

Baylor scores a parking spot right out front of our favorite café, Sassafras. This place has the most amazing French toast, which is fantabulous because I'm starving. Food is all I seem to think about these days but food is a good comfort right now. It can't hurt me, well unless I get diabetes it could, but life surely couldn't be that cruel to kick a woman when she's already down.

With our bellies full, Baylor and I walk down the street and enter Nordstrom's. We head to the women's department and begin looking. Bay finds a stunning purple—no surprises there—dress that has no pockets but it looks amazing on her, so she grabs it.

I have a pile of clothes and I'm happy with my haul. I've just pulled my dress back on when a stabbing pain rips through my abdomen, I double over and grunt in pain. "You okay, Charli?" Baylor sings out.

Opening the cubicle door, I look up at her and shake my head. "Bay, something's wrong."

DOMINIC 22

It's still radio silence from Charli and I'm starting to get worried. It's not like her to ignore me and not return my calls or texts. No one in the office has heard from her, and Corey is being a right royal cocksucker to me at the moment.

The mail guy knocks on my door and hands me an envelope. I stare at the orange rectangle in my hands. My name is scrawled on the front; no other postmarks or details give me any clue as to whom it's from. Sliding my finger under the flap, I open it and pull out a single card, it falls from my fingers to my desk. Picking it, confusion once again mars my face and I scrunch it up as I read the card.

MANHATTAN VAULTS

VAULTS 154, 155 & 176

"If the wind changes, your face will stay like that," Elena says from the doorway.

"Har har, very funny," I say. "What are you doing here?"

"Thought I'd stop by before my ER shift and see how you're doing. It's been a few days and I thought you would have called me with an update."

"I have no news, I haven't spoken to Charli."

"Why not?" she sasses, as she takes the seat across from me.

"She's not answering my calls."

"Have you been to her place?" I nod. "Have you made a grand gesture so she knows you're thinking of her?"

"I punched the dick that's making her life hell right now and broke his nose."

"And they say chivalry is dead. But seriously, Big Bro, I think you need to up your game in the romance department. FYI, punches aren't really all that sexy to a woman."

"I think I have a lead to clear her name…but it means I have to go to New York."

"Then you better book flight to The Big Apple. I wanna meet the lucky lady who has your balls in a twist."

"Please never refer to my balls, or them being in a twist ever again."

"But it's ohh so fun teasing you, Brother."

"Lucky I love you."

"You have no choice."

"That's debatable."

"Got time for a coffee?"

"Always for my pain in the ass little sister."

Placing the card back in the envelope, I slip it into my drawer and grab my wallet. Slinging my arm around her shoulder, we exit my office. We run into Corey on the way to the elevators and the look he gives me is murderous.

"Corey, this is—"

"Don't care," he snarls, "How many do you have on the go?" Then he quietly mumbles, "She's fuckin' better off without you."

Before I can ask him for clarification, he storms away. Leaving me even more confused.

"He seems nice," Elena says, as we enter the metal car.

"He normally is but his fiancée is a bit of a loose cannon from what I've heard around the office."

"That's no reason to be a dick monkey."

"Dick monkey? You been speaking with Abi?"

"Yeah, I think she's lonely now that we're both no longer in town."

"Maybe she can visit over spring break."

"I think she'd like that. You think Mom and Dad will let her?"

"So they can have alone time? Hell yes."

She laughs as we reach the ground floor. We walk through the foyer and across the street to the coffee shop. She grabs a table and I go order. While waiting I grab my phone and try Charli but like usual, she sends me to voice-mail. "Hey, Angel. It's me. Again. Please let me know you're okay. Love you."

I'm starting to get worried. I really need to get this accusation quashed so Charli can come back to work and I can see her again. I miss her like crazy.

My name is called, snapping me back to the present. I grab our coffees and join Elena at the table she snagged.

After our catch-up, I head back to the office and grab the envelope. Pulling out the card, I read it again. Waking my computer, I pull up Google and search Manhattan Vaults. Dialing the number it rings a few times, "Manhattan Vaults, this is Lana, how may I help you?"

"I'm chasing information on box 154?" I'll start with the first number and go from there.

"Certainly, let me look that up." I can hear keys tapping in the background. "Okay, Mr. Davis, how can I assist you today?"

"I'm sorry, did you just say Davis?"

"Are you not Dean Davis?" she questions, her voice pitches high but not in that 'I just fucked up way.' I can't put my finger on it but she seems almost happy that she was discovered. Disconnecting the call, I grab the card, stand up, and exit my office. I make my way to the boss's office and knock. "You got a minute, Boss Lady?" I ask her.

She glares at me and points to the seat across from her. "Of course."

Entering, I take a seat and hand the card to her. "This was delivered to me earlier today. It's to do with Charli's predicament."

"That's a big leap."

"Well, when I called them, the lady who answered called me Mr. Davis when I gave the first box number, and when I questioned my name she called me Dean Davis."

Her eyes widen. "So much for security but that is quite the coincidence, no wonder IA think she's involved."

"I know, right? Is this enough to get a warrant to get access to the vault and their records?"

"No, but I would like you to head to New York and see what you can garner in person. This could be what we need to clear Charli and nail Dean further to the wall."

Nodding, I stand up. "I'll be on the next flight."

"Keep me posted and, Dominic," I look back to her, "don't tell anyone about this."

"You got it."

Exiting her office, I head back to mine and I book an American Airlines flight leaving O'Hare at four thirty this afternoon. Shutting down, I grab my laptop and things and head home to pack for my flight.

After checking in, I make my way to the departure lounge. A loved-up couple sits across from me and my mind drifts to Charli. I wish she was coming with me. This time of year is always magical in New York, maybe once all this shit is over, she and I can go on a trip somewhere together. But in order for that to happen, I need to clear her name, and I'll stop at nothing to do that.

Charli is worth going to hell and back for. I've fallen hard for her and I'm not letting her go.

BAY RACES ME TO WESTERN GENERAL, I'M PRETTY SURE SHE broke several laws on the way here, but I'm fine with that because I'm really worried right now. She parks her car in the emergency lot and when we enter the ER, she goes all Bitchy Baylor and makes a scene. She's yell that she's Dr. Flynn Kelly's sister-in-law and that I need to be seen straightaway because it's life or death. I wouldn't go that far but as soon as she says I'm pregnant, they sure change their tune.

I'm escorted back to a cubicle where they take my vitals. A doctor pulls back the curtain, she looks to me and smiles. Her eyes look familiar but I haven't seen her before. "I'm Elena, what seems to be the issue?"

"I—"

But Bay interrupts me, "We were shopping and Charli made a sound like a pig dying and when I opened the door she was huddled over and looked like shit." She looks to me. "Sorry, but you did." She turns back to the doctor. "I hauled ass here. Now please tell me that this lil' bubba is okay, my girl here doesn't need any more shit to happen. I know they say things come in threes, but we don't need a third shit thing to happen."

"Would you mind getting a lemonade?" the doctor asks Bay.

"Yep, sure, no worries." She turns to me. "Be right back."

She exits the room leaving me with the doctor. "She's kinda full-on," she says to me.

"She's Baylor. She marches to the beat of her own drum."

She laughs and nods. "Well, now that it's just us. You want to tell me what happened?"

"She pretty much said it all. We had brunch. Then went shopping. I was changing back into my dress when a stabbing pain ripped through me. I've never felt anything like it before."

"And how far along are you?"

"Almost ten weeks."

She nods. "Let me grab the Doppler and I'll check the baby's heartbeat and then we can get you a scan. If you can, change into the gown and then hop up on the bed. I'll be back in a sec."

Nodding my head, I take a deep breath and take the gown from her. I change into the gown and climb onto the bed. Lying back, I stare up at the ceiling and close my eyes. They pop wide open when I hear someone say, "Dr. Cruz, where did you want the ultrasound machine?"

Dr. Cruz, shit, she's Nic's sister. The curtain pulls back and it's Bay. "I need to get out of here," I tell her.

"Did the doctor give you the all clear?"

Shaking my head, *no*, I whisper-shout, "She's Nic's sister."

"No fucking way?" she screeches in surprise. "There's your third thing." She looks to me wide eyed. "You don't think she knows who you are?"

"I don't think so. He's mentioned me but there's a million Charli's out there, I could be anyone."

"How do you know she's his sister?"

"Someone called her Dr. Cruz."

"Maybe there's a million Dr. Cruzes out there?"

"No, this is karma biting me in my fat pregnant ass for lying and keeping this from him."

"You haven't lied. You just haven't been honest." I raise my eyebrows at her, "Okay, well, yeah, it's kinda sorta a lie."

"I'm so screwed," I cry.

The curtain to my cubicle is pulled back and a male doctor is standing there. He steps into the area. "Hey, Flynn," Baylor says to him, wrapping her arms around him for a hug.

"Baylor, I hear you caused a scene on arrival."

"Charli needed a doctor and you're the best I know. Actually, Preston would be better. He deals with kids, can you get Preston?"

"He deals with children, last I checked Charli is an adult."

"But her baby isn't."

"You're pregnant?" he asks me.

"Almost ten weeks along," I say, nodding and shuffling into a sitting position.

"Very well—"

"Can you treat me? I'm sure Dr. Cruz is good, but I'd prefer if you saw me."

"Can I ask why?"

Biting my lip, I stare at him. My mouth opens and closes a few times, I don't know how to voice this, but thankfully, Baylor does it for me. "The baby daddy is Dr. Cruz's brother. He doesn't know yet and to be honest, he doesn't deserve to know because he's a jerkface cockwank."

"And why is he a jerkface cockwank, as you put it?"

"He told another chick to deal with her pregnancy herself, he don't want to play daddy."

"Ouch," Flynn says. "Leave it with me and I'll take over."

"Thank you," I quietly say.

He exits again and leaves me with Bay. "Thank you," I tell her, "I appreciate you getting Flynn to take over my case."

"Anytime, but what's the point in knowing people in high places if you can't call on them in a time of need?"

"You really are a bitch," I tell her.

"Once a bitch, always a bitch," she says with a shrug and drops onto the end of my bed, and to be honest, I wouldn't have her any other way. Baylor is Baylor and I'm so glad to have her on my team right now. I think I'll be needing her more than ever in the coming months.

Three hours later, Baylor is fluffing my pillows at home, my home. I got the all clear from Flynn, everything is okay with the baby, but my blood pressure is a little elevated. He recommends I take it easy and thinks I need to tell Dominic about the baby. I know he's right but I don't think I'm emotionally ready to hear him tell me what he told that woman. I don't think I'll ever be ready to hear those words, but Flynn's right, he needs to know. Taking a deep breath, I dial his number.

My heart races as it rings. "Charli," he says when he answers, "I don't have time to talk. I'll call you soon." And he hangs up, without letting me get a word in.

His actions crush me and only cement to me that I, no we, are better off alone and without him. Rolling to my side, I curl into a ball and begin to cry. Through my tears, I wail, "Falling for Agent Cruz was the dumbest thing I ever did."

DOMINIC 24

Of course Charli calls me just as I've boarded my connecting flight. Yes, in my rush, I booked a flight via Charlotte with a one-hour layover, and due to bad weather, that layover time has doubled. I quickly tell her I can't talk and hang up. After the death stare of all death stares from the stewardess, I pocket my phone with the intention of calling her first thing tomorrow morning, because it will be close to midnight before I get to my hotel.

The landing in LaGuardia is bumpy and after what feels like a million hours, I finally make it to my hotel. Collapsing onto the bed, I fall asleep immediately.

The blaring of my alarm wakes me. It feels like I only just went to sleep a few moments ago, but I've been asleep for nearly six hours. It's just before seven, still too early to call Charli so I decide to go for a run. With my headphones in, I head toward Central Park. It's absolutely gorgeous here this time of year, actually, I love New York any time of the year. It's a great place to visit but I could never see myself living here. It's too peopley.

Heading back to the hotel, I grab a shower and decide to head straight to Manhattan Vaults. The sooner I can get the proof I need, the sooner I can clear Charli's name and life can get back to normal. Well, a new normal because I plan on living life to the fullest, with Charli by my side. I want to grow old and wrinkly with this woman. I want to see her stomach swell as our future babies grow inside her. I want to travel the world with her by my side, I want it all with her. She's it for me.

Pushing open the brass door, I step into the opulent reception area of Manhattan Vaults. It's such a pompous place but I will admit, the security is top-notch. I walk toward the front desk and I'm greeted by a woman with pink hair. I see her name tag says 'Lana.' She's the lady I spoke to yesterday.

"Welcome to Manhattan Vaults, how can I help you?"

"Hi, I'm hoping you can help me, Lana. I'm Agent Dominic Cruz from Chicago. I'm looking into a case and Manhattan Vaults came up. I was hoping I can get details on three of your vaults."

"We take security and privacy here very seriously, Agent Cruz. Unless you have a warrant, we will be unable to assist you." She's acting more professional than she did yesterday. I can't gauge if this is all a ruse or if she really is following protocol and yesterday was just a slip of the tongue."

"Is there a manager I can speak to? This is of grave importance and time is of the essence."

"I will see if Mr. Anders is available to see you, but I assure you, he will tell you exactly the same."

Leaning on the counter, I stare down at her. I'm about

to play hardball and Lana here won't know what hit her. "I'm sure Mr. Anders would be interested to know that you, Lana, confirmed the name on an account to me over the phone without verifying whom I was." Her eyes widen. "In case you're confused, I'm not the account holder. I think Mr. Anders would be very interested to hear about that security breach."

Her eyes dart around. "Please, I'm sure I can assist you without really breaking any privacy rules." She glances around again, and then whispers, "I can't get you access to the vaults, but I'm more than happy to give you names and entry records."

"That would be wonderful, Lana."

"What are the vault numbers?"

"I'm interested in vaults 154, 155, and 176."

"Give me a few moments to bring it all up."

"Thank you, Lana. I appreciate your help."

Ten minutes later, I'm on my way back to my hotel with a folder of paperwork to go through. Stopping at a coffee shop, I grab a coffee and sandwich. With food in hand, I head to the hotel and up to my room.

Sitting on the bed, I begin to read everything that Lana gave me. My eyes widen as I read, this isn't enough to clear Charli but it's enough to cause doubt. I need to get back to Chicago and pay Dean a visit.

"You again," he smartly says as he's escorted into the room. The guard removes his cuffs and he sits across from me. This guy really is an asshole.

"Thought I'd pay you a visit, Dean Davis." His eyes widen when I use that name.

"I think you have the wrong person, my name is Dean Chikatilo."

"Not according to paperwork at Manhattan Vaults."

"How the fuck do you know about that?"

"I'll be asking the questions here, asshole. Does Charli know you were using her as a cover for your laundering?"

"How the fuck did you figure this all out?"

"I didn't, but you just confirmed my suspicions." His eyes widen again. "When I discovered you were using the name Dean Davis, it expanded my searches. You'd be surprised at what I found…but then again, I don't think you would be since you and your brother are the masterminds behind this. The only thing that confuses me is, why did you to get involved with Kye Vlahos?"

"I ain't telling you shit. If you had anything solid, it wouldn't be you here interrogating me."

"Ohh believe me, they will be. I just wanted to confirm for myself before I hand all this over, but I do have one question, I—"

"I ain't telling you shit."

"I want to know why you bought Charli into this."

"It's always about her. That bitch can never do anything wrong. She's like Mary-fucking-Poppins, always cheery. She can do no wrong. Everyone loves her but she never…"

"Never what?"

"It doesn't matter because when I go down, she goes down. Collateral damage as such."

Shaking my head, I stare at him. "This isn't over, Chikatilo, mark my words, you and your brother are going down."

"And Charli will come with us."

"Not if I can help it."

Standing up, I exit the room. Closing the door behind me, I lean back, close my eyes, and exhale deeply.

"What are you doing here?" a voice says from my left.

Turning my head, I look over and see Corey Cox. "Fuck," I mumble, "trying to clear Charli's name."

"Like you care about her."

"What's that supposed to mean?"

"Don't play dumb, Cruz. Just leave her alone. She's better off without you."

"Why do I get the feeling you know something that I don't?"

"Wow, very astute of you. Just leave her alone."

He shoves me in the shoulder as he storms off. Shaking my head, I stare at his retreating form and I play his words over and over. I feel like I'm missing something, but what?

Climbing into my car, I drive straight to the office. Making my way upstairs, I head to Amanda's office. She makes time for me and I fill her in on everything I've discovered. "Visiting Dean was stupid, Dominic. We've now lost the element of surprise."

"But it proves Charli is innocent," I tell her.

"It won't be enough for IA. We need solid evidence that Charli had nothing to do with any of this." She pauses. "Do you think you can get the sign in/out paperwork for the vaults? If we can prove that Charli isn't associated with the vault and it was Darren and Dean who set it up, that should be enough."

"Not without a warrant. Had Lana not messed up when I called, she wouldn't have given me what I got."

"Leave it with me. I'll reach out to a colleague and see what we can come up with. Good work, Dominic. Make sure to tell Charli all of this. Won't be long and her smiling face will be back in the halls here."

"Will do."

Leaving Amanda's office, I decide to head over to Charli's place. I've missed seeing her and I really want to give her this news in person. I'm stuck in traffic when my phone rings. "Branson, what's up?"

"Just checking to see where you are? Kasey and I are waiting for you."

"Shit," I remark, "I totally forgot, give me twenty and I'll be there."

"Sure, no worries. See you soon."

Changing my destination, I head to Bin 501 for dinner with Branson and Kasey. It's been great reconnecting with him since moving here, and Kasey, she's just a gem. I still can't believe they are together but if I'm honest, I always saw a spark between them but Kody swooped in first and won the girl. I still can't believe he's gone but as the saying goes 'the good die young' and Kody definitely falls into that category. However, in saying that, had he not passed Kasey and Branson never would have gotten together, he'd never do that to his brother.

Traffic is much lighter heading this way and I arrive at Branson's wine bar quite quickly. Walking inside, I smile when I see Branson, but I'm stopped in my tracks when a blonde bombshell slaps me across the cheek. "You're a fucking dick," she snarls at me.

Rubbing my cheek, I take a good look at her and then I register that it's Baylor, Charli's best friend and Corey's fiancée.

"Nice to see you again too. Mind telling me why you slapped me?"

"Mind telling me why you're a fucking dickwad?"

"Watch your mouth, Kitten," Corey says, running his palm down her upper arm.

"He deserves every curse word I'm spewing for what he's done."

"What have I done?" I ask, genuinely confused.

"You really are a piece of work. Charli doesn't need you in her life."

"Is Charli okay?"

"Like you care. Where have you been?"

"New York. I'm following a lead to clear her name."

This stops her in her tracks. "Ohh, well that's good, but what about your baby? You going to step up to the plate and be a father?"

"What baby?"

"Your baby, you told your baby momma to fuck off."

"I did," I confirm. "But—"

"But nothing, you need to be there for your baby, dickwad."

"It's. Not. My. Baby," I say through gritted teeth.

"Of course you'd say that. Men always say that." She looks to Corey. "But not you, you're amazing. You'd never do that." She looks back to me. "Unlike this dickwad."

"The baby isn't mine…hang on, how do you know about this?"

"Charli heard you telling her you want nothing to do with your baby."

"I said that because it isn't mine. My ex got pregnant by the guy she cheated on me with. He dumped her and she came crawling back to me."

"Ohh," she says, her eyes widen. "Ohhhhhhh, shit. You really need to tell Charli this."

"I plan on seeing her later, if I can find her. She's been on my mind all week and it's killing me not seeing her.

Since she was suspended she's been ghosting me. I miss her. I love her. I only went to New York for her."

Baylor looks to Corey and mumbles, "This is a big pile of shit."

"Why do I get the feeling there's more to this big pile of shit, as you so put it?"

"Because there is more, but you need turn around and go find Charli, and you need to go find her now and sort all this out."

"Is she okay?"

A smile graces her face. "She will be now."

"Everything all right?" Branson asks, as he walks over to us.

"I have no clue," I tell him.

"It will be, once he gets to his girl." She's now calm, her demeanor just now reminds me of Jekyll and Hyde. "You need to leave, now."

Looking to Branson, I ask, "Can we get a rain check? I need to get to my girl. I don't know why but I just know I need to see her."

"Of course. Call me later and fill me in."

Nodding my head, I exit the restaurant and head back to my car. I climb in, start the engine, and gun it. I need to get to Charli and I need to get to her now.

CHARLI 25

BAY AND COREY JUST LEFT, THEY INVITED ME TO GO WITH them to Bin 501 but A. I don't feel like going out, and B. That's where I met *him* and I'm trying to forget about *him* right now. I finally reach out and he shuts me down, promising to call, and days later it's radio silence from him. This is what I get for reaching out, well screw him. This baby and I don't need a dickwad like him around.

Turning on the TV, I bring up Netflix and start watching *Prison Break* because hello, Wentworth Miller and Dominic Purcell. After three episodes my eyes become heavy so I turn everything off and head to bed. I've just crawled under the covers when I hear a knock at my apartment door. I'm pretty sure I know who it is but I don't have the energy right now to deal with *him,* so I lay here. Ignoring the banging and pleading from Nic.

Knocking.

Silence.

"Please, Charli, open up."

Silence.

"I love you and miss you."

Silence.

"Please open up, Angel. I need to see you."

Silence.

"Please."

Silence.

More knocking.

"I know you can hear me, I'm going to go now but just know I love you, and I'll be back tomorrow."

Silence.

"Angel, I will be back morning, noon, and night until you open up and talk to me because," pause, "I love you, Charli Davis."

Silence.

Closing my eyes, I take a deep breath and decide it's time to face him. I shuffle though my apartment but when I open the door, he's not there. I step into the hallway and look both ways but it's empty. "Dammit," I mumble to myself, as I close the door and head back to bed. Just as I snuggle in, my phone pings with a text. Opening the message, I read it.

NIC: *Please just let me know you're okay. I miss you and love you, Charli Davis. That will never change. NEVER. I'll be back tomorrow and every day until you see me. You are it for me, Angel. I love you to the moon and back.*

My eyes well with tears as I read his message. "But will you still love me when I tell you I'm pregnant?" I tearfully mumble to the room.

Rolling to my side, I cry myself to sleep.

Waking the next morning, I feel like shit and for once, it's not from my pregnancy. I feel like shit because I miss Nic more than anything in the world. I'm a hormonal emotional mess right now. A run will help clear my mind so I hop up, change into my running gear, and set off to reinvigorate my soul and clear my mind.

Unfortunately for me, neither of those things occur. If anything, my run only made things worse. It gave me time to think, and thinking isn't good right now because my mind runs wild, really wild, and it's also playing tricks on me. I feel like I'm being watched.

Taking a seat on a nearby bench, I bend down to fake retie my laces and I covertly look around. Nothing seems out of place, clearly my mind is playing tricks on me. Sitting back up, I realize that I'm hungry, and then I start thinking of a cheeseburger. I eat at least one a day right now.

Standing up, I take one last glance around and when I don't see anything suspicious, I jog to the closest McDonald's and order a cheeseburger meal. Sitting down, I devour my meal and then I order two more. Hey, sue me, I'm pregnant.

With my belly full, I make my way home and that feeling of being watched hits me again, but this time when I look around, I see a van that heightens my unease. The driver and I make eye contact, this causes their eyes to widen and they quickly drive off. "That was weird," I tell myself, and I continue to make my way home.

When I step inside my apartment, I get the feeling that someone has been here. Nothing appears to be out of place but the air has a smell to it that wasn't here before I left. Walking into my room, I strip off my clothes and climb into the shower. The hot water feels amazing on my muscles. Soaping up my hands, I wash myself. My breasts are very sensitive at the moment and when I brush over them, I moan. My whole body comes alive in a way that only Nic has ever pulled from me.

Closing my eyes, I run my hands over my stomach and I slide down farther, between my thighs. Spreading my legs, I slip my finger between my folds and shudder when I touch my clit. Circling my finger around the sensitive bundle, I massage my breast with my other hand. Pleasure builds down low, my breathing picks up as I continue to twist and rub myself. Sliding my finger down, I press my digit inside of me. Hitting the bundle of joy within. Inserting another finger, I pump my fingers in and out. Twisting my finger, hitting that magic spot each time, I moan Nic's name as I come. My body trembling at the intensity of my climax.

Pulling my fingers out, I turn around and slide down the wall. Tears stream down my face. "I miss you, Nic," I blubber. Resting my head on my knees I cry, wishing he was by my side and kicking myself for not answering the door last night.

Deciding I need to speak to him, I hop out and dry off. I pull on a cute sundress and apply a little makeup. Grabbing my purse, I head down to my car and drive over to Nic's place. Taking a deep breath, I walk up his front stairs and knock.

But I'm met with silence.

Turning around, I walk back to my car, hop in, and dejectedly I drive back home. Stripping off my dress, I pull on my sweatpants and FBI hoodie. Grabbing a pint of Ben and Jerry's, I collapse onto the sofa and watch more *Prison Break*.

My phone rings and I look down to see it's Baylor. "Hey, Bay," I quietly say.

"Hey hey, sexy lady," she cheerfully says. "What you doing?"

"Eating ice cream and watching *Prison Break*."

"Ohh, Wentworth Miller. Totally sucks that he's gay."

"Yep," I reply, letting the 'P' pop.

"Well, since you aren't doing anything. Come on over for dinner. Corey cooked waaaaay too much and if I eat all of this, I'll end up fat."

"Bay, I really don't feel like going out again."

"Well, that's too bad. You need to stop moping and get on with life. Get your ass over here now or I will…"

"Will what?"

"I don't know but I will do something that gets you over here."

"You aren't going to give up until I agree, are you?"

"You know me too well," she cheekily says, "See you within the hour."

"I hate you," I tell her.

"Love/hate, same-same. See you soon."

Huffing I stand up. I look at what I'm wearing and consider changing back into my dress from earlier, but Bay is making me go against my wishes so I don't care that I look like a homeless slob. At least my hair and makeup is still on point.

Once again, I grab my purse and head down to my car and head over to Bay's place.

Knocking on the door, I wait for Bay to answer. I grab my phone and see that I have no new texts from Nic. The door swings open and Bay looks me up and down. "Glad to see you dressed up for the occasion."

"Bite me" I tell her, and the bitch does exactly that. "Did you just bite me?"

"You told me to," she says with a shrug.

"It's a figure of speech, you bitch."

"Whatevs, come on, the food is getting cold."

We walk inside and when I step into the kitchen my eyes widen when I see who's standing next to Corey. "Nic, what are you doing here?"

DOMINIC 26

Leaving Charli's place just now killed me. Knowing she was inside but not answering really hurt me. Something is going on, I can feel it in my bones. I need her to know that I'm here so I send her a text. I lay it all out for her, telling her she's it for me via text isn't the most romantic way to do it, but I need her to know how deeply I care for her. I know it's only been a few months but when you know you know. It was the same for Mom and Dad, and it seems, well I hope, it's also the case for Charli and me.

Pulling away from her place, I notice a van across the street. Seems a bit late for a delivery but then again, I'm not a delivery worker, I don't know what hours they keep.

Making my way home, I head inside and collapse onto my sofa. I stare up at the ceiling and think about the last time that Charli and I were here…

.   .   .

...We have just cleaned up the dinner dishes. Charli cooked me an amazing risotto dish and we washed it down with a lovely red. With our wine glasses in hand, we are now snuggling on the sofa watching a movie. It feels very domesticated and I laugh.

"What's got you giggling?" she asks, looking up at me.

"This feels all domesticated." I pause. "It's perfect."

"It sure is perfect and you know why?"

"Why?"

She sits up, takes my wine from me and places our drinks on the coffee table. She straddles my lap and stares into my eyes. "It's because you are perfect, Dominic Cruz."

"I think you have that the wrong way around, YOU are perfect, Charli Davis. You are perfect in every way."

Gripping her cheeks in my palms I press my lips to hers. She places her hands over mine and kisses me back. Our tongues languidly slide in and out of each other's mouths. My cock hardens between us, there's no way she can't feel how hard I am. She breaks our kiss and shimmies back along my thighs and drops to the floor. She makes quick work of my button and before I can process what's happening, her lips wrap around my cock and she sucks.

"Fuuuuck," I moan, and she continues to blow me. "Your mouth feels sooo good but you know what's better?"

"What?" she huskily asks.

"Your pussy."

Lifting her back onto my lap, I'm glad she's wearing a dress because I can't wait. I shove the material up, pull her panties to the side and thrust my hips upward.

"Nnnnniic," she moans.

She holds on to my shoulders and rides me. Our eyes are steadfastly locked on one another as she goes to town on my cock. She meets me thrust for thrust and together we reach our peak. Grunting and growling through our release.

She rests for forehead against mine. Our breathing hurried. "I love you, Nic."

"I love you too, Angel."

...as that memory fades, I realize my cock is just as hard now as it was then. As much as I want to pleasure myself right now, I want to save my release for Charli. She owns them, just like she owns my heart.

Standing up, I walk into my bedroom and strip off, heading into my bathroom for a cold shower to ease my cock. It doesn't work though because memories of Charli and I assault me while I'm in here, and I can't help myself. I grip my cock and pump vigorously. Sooner than a grown man should, I spray my cum all over the shower wall.

After my self-love, I wash myself and climb out. Drying off, I slip into bed naked, and drift off to sleep where I dream inappropriate sexy things about Charli and me.

When I wake the next morning, I decide to head into the office to see if I can find out anything more about Darren and Dean Chikatilo. Grabbing my helmet, I ride my bike, hoping the freedom of the ride will clear my head, plus it will soon be too icy and dangerous to ride so I'll take the opportunity while I can.

Parking my bike, I make my way to the elevator, pushing the call button, I wait. The doors open and Baylor and Corey exit.

"Hey," I offer in greeting.

"Morning," Corey says.

"Hey," Baylor enthusiastically says. "How did it go last night?"

"It didn't."

"What do you mean it didn't?" she snaps at me, her voice laced with anger. If looks could kill, I'd be six feet under right now.

"Calm down, Kitten," Corey placates her.

"I went to her place but she wasn't there, or she was ignoring me. I really don't think she wants to see me."

"She does," Bay assures me, "she just needs to pull her head out of her ass." She pauses. "Do you trust me?"

I eye her, I don't know this woman from a bar of soap, but for some reason I do trust her when it comes to Charli. "Can't believe I'm saying this, but yes, I do trust you."

"Then be at our place tonight and leave the rest to me."

"What are you planning?" Corey asks her.

"I'm planning on getting my best friend and this dude back together again."

"We didn't break up," I tell her.

"Semantics. Just be at our place tonight and I will make sure she's there so you guys can clear the air and get back on the same page 'cause right now, you are in two different chapters and I need you guys to get your HEA."

"What's a HEA?"

"Duh, it's a Happily Ever After. If anyone deserves it, it's my girl Charli and she just so happens to deserve her HEA with you. Now, our place tonight." She smiles at me and walks off, leaving Corey and me alone.

"Should I be worried?" I ask him.

"When it comes to her," he nods his head toward her, "definitely."

"Thanks, I think."

He slaps me on the shoulder and walks over to Baylor. He scoops her over his shoulder and she squeals. She slaps him on the ass and he returns the favor. I smile watching them. I want that for Charli and me…and maybe after tonight I will get it.

After reaching several dead ends, I look up and realize it's 4:00 p.m. already. Shutting down my computer, I make my way over to Baylor and Corey's place. She smiles when she sees me. "You need to hide you bike."

"Does Charli not know I'm coming?"

"Ummm."

"Please tell me she knows."

"Ummm, she knows." I go to tell her I'm leaving when she grabs my arm, digging her nails in. "Please stay. I know deep down she wants to see you but she's, well, she needs to see you, and this is the only way I can think to get her here. Now that you're here, I can get her here without it looking suspicious."

"Fine," I relent. "But if she's pissed, I'm leaving after I tell her this was all your idea. I don't want to cause her any anguish."

"Trust me, you won't. Now move the bike and I'll message Charli."

"Are you sure this is going to be okay, Baylor? I really don't think she wants to see me," I question Baylor again, still not comfortable about being here.

"She needs to see you." She keeps saying that, but why?

"Can't you just tell me why she needs to see me?"

"Nope, not my place, just trust me."

Again, she keeps saying that but before I can wonder any more, there's a knock at the front door. She's here. Nerves rack through my body as I wait for Baylor to answer the door and let my Angel in.

CHARLI 27

I'M GOING TO KILL MY EX-BEST FRIEND, I THINK TO MYSELF AS I stare at Nic standing before me. Why is she meddling? Why is he here? And why is he so fucking sexy? If we weren't currently standing in Corey and Bay's living room, I'd totally mount him like the stallion that he is. *Damn pregnancy hormones.*

"Hi, Angel," he says, even his voice is divine.

"Hi," I hesitantly say, "what are you doing here?"

"I've missed seeing your beautiful face."

"You have?"

"Yes."

That one word shoots straight to my heart. My eyes water and then Baylor says a sentence that causes my eyes to pop wide open.

"Wow, those pregnancy hormones have turned you soft, you're crying again."

"Pregnancy hormones?" Nic questions.

"Oops," Bay says, and for the first time since knowing

her, she seems shocked at what just came out of her mouth.

"You're pregnant?" he asks, and my head nods on its own. I wait for him to tell me to go to hell and it's not his blah blah blah, but he doesn't. "You're pregnant? With my baby?" Words once again elude me and I nod.

He's silent, his eyes keep darting from my belly to my face and then the biggest smile graces his face. "We're having a baby." It's not a question, it's a statement and I realize he's happy.

"You're okay with this?" I question.

"Absolutely. We're having a baby," he says again. He steps to me and takes my hands in his. "Why didn't you tell me?"

"I heard you with Bianca the other day and—"

He cups my cheek in his palm and shakes his head, "Her baby isn't mine."

"It isn't?"

"Nope. It's Lawrence's." My eyes widen.

"Ohh shit, I've made such a mess of things."

"How so?"

"I thought you didn't want to have anything to do with her baby, and I freaked out thinking you'd react the same way when I told you. So I pushed you away because I couldn't deal with heartache like that."

"You weren't going to tell me about the baby?"

"I was, eventually. I was just trying to deal with the prospect of doing this solo." I stare up into his chocolate brown orbs. "I should have known there was more to it. I know you. I know you wouldn't turn your back on your baby. Please forgive me for doubting you."

"There's nothing to forgive. Given what you heard, I understand why you thought what you did. Does it hurt that you thought that? Yes, but I've heard pregnancy hormones are crazy so no apology is necessary. Just know, Charli Davis, I will be by your side every step of the way." He places emphasis on the last five words.

"Really?" I question again.

"Really, really." Not giving me a chance to question or protest, he presses his lips to mine, reaffirming his love for me...and our baby.

"Fuck me," Baylor says from beside us, "I think I just got pregnant from that kiss."

"Watch your mouth, Kitten," Corey says, "Let's give these two some privacy."

"Piss off, I want to watch the Charli and Nic show."

"Dominic," Nic growls at Bay.

"How come she gets to call you Nic?"

"Because she's the mother of my child."

"That's pregnancy prejudice and one-hundred-percent not fair."

Corey shakes his head, takes Bay's hand in his, and drags her protesting from the room.

"Are you sure?" I ask him again, still amazed he wants me and the baby.

He nods his head at me. "You are everything I need and more, Angel."

"You have that the wrong way around, Nic. I need you. We need you. This baby needs you."

"And you have me. I'm sorry that you misunderstood what I said to Bianca. I would never turn my back on my child. Momma would have my ass if I did."

A laugh escapes me. "Your momma sounds amazing."

"She is and she's going to be stoked to become a γιαγιά."

"Yeay whata?"

"Γιαγιά. It's Greek for grandma."

"Γιαγιά, I like it. What's grandad?"

"Pappoús but my dad will go by Papa, just like his and so on."

"I love that."

"What will your parents want to be called?"

"Granny and Grumpy." He laughs and it's a deep belly laugh.

"Grumpy, really?"

"It's totally an affectionate term."

"Well, I love that too. Sounds like this little one will be spoiled by his or her grandparents."

"And her aunty," Baylor says, handing me a gift bag.

"What's this?" I ask.

"Open it and find out."

Pulling out the tissue paper I find three items. I pull them out and lay them on the back of the sofa since it's the closest surface. There are three shirts with Daddy Agent, Mommy Agent, and Baby Agent printed on them.

"Turn them over," Bay says.

On the back is #TeamCruz with the number three.

"Bay," I cry, "this is amazing." Throwing my arms around her, I hug her to me and whisper, "Thank you."

"You are welcome. Just remember that Baylor is a great girl's name." I laugh. "I'm serious. At least gimme the middle name since I sorted this all out for you."

We all laugh at Baylor but from the look on her face, she's deadly serious. "How about Nic and I have a name chat first."

"Fine," she huffs. "Let's pop some bubbly to celebrate."

"Mean much?" I tease her.

"Name her Baylor and we will all have grape juice with you."

Again, we all laugh and head into the kitchen to get drinks. The guys have beer, Bay has bubbly, and I have grape juice. "To baby Cruz," Corey says.

"To baby Cruz," we all echo. The guys head outside to start the grill, while Bay and I stay inside to finish prepping the meat and salad.

"Grill's ready," Corey yells.

Since I'm closest to the meat tray, I grab it and head outside when I overhear Corey. "I owe you an apology, Cruz."

This causes me to pause. "Why?"

"I've been a dick to you all week, thinking you'd turned your back on Charli. I guess we all judged before having the whole story."

"If the shoe was on the other foot, I would have jumped to the same conclusion. But I meant what I said before, I will be there any way that she'll have me."

"She wants you by her side," I say, stepping outside.

Handing the meat to Corey, I walk over to Nic, and slide my arm around his waist. "I mean it, Nic. We need and want you by our side."

"And I want to be there. Every step of the way."

Lifting to my tippy-toes, I press my lips to his. My pregnancy hormones decide to wave and shake their jazz hands on my clit, and I unabashedly moan into the kiss, rubbing myself on his leg to ease the friction currently pinging between my thighs.

"You getting a clit boner?" Bay asks, as she places the salads on the table.

"A what?" I ask, pulling away from Nic and blushing at my brazenness.

"A clit boner?" I scrunch my eyes in confusion. "You know, when your clit tingles and grows, a clit boner."

Shaking my head, I laugh. "I'm not answering that."

"That's totally a yes," she says. "You guys alright for drinks?"

They both nod their heads indicating they are good. She heads back inside and returns a few moments later with a wine bucket and her drink. In the bucket is her bubbly and my grape juice.

The four of us have a chillaxed and quiet evening. It's the most content I've felt since I discovered I was pregnant. We laughed. We—well they—got drunk but most of all, Nic was by my side.

Later that evening, I fold a drunk Nic into my car and drive back to my place. He and I make it upstairs and we fall into bed. Lying in Nic's arm, I have a smile on my face. This is the first time in days that I feel happy and content. No longer do I think falling for Agent Cruz is bad, falling for Daddy Cruz is the best thing I've ever done.

DOMINIC 28

WHEN I WAKE UP, I REALIZE IT WASN'T A DREAM. I'M IN BED with Charli and she's snuggled into my side. I have the hangover from hell—remind me never to go shot for shot with Baylor again. Now I know why Corey said no.

"Ugh," I groan.

"Feeling a little under the weather?" Charli asks me, lifting her head to stare up at me. Her chin resting on my pec.

"Why didn't you warn me about Baylor?"

"'Cause everyone needs to at least once go shot for shot with her. You are officially a team member now."

"I like being a part of Team Davis."

"And I like being on Team Cruz." I pause and smile. "I can't believe Baylor got us #TeamCruz shirts."

"She really is something else."

"She's Baylor. You either love her or loathe her."

"Well, I know I love you, Charli Davis, and I'm never letting you go."

"Is that so?" she says, as she straddles me, rubbing herself on my growing cock. It's then I realize we're naked and I wonder if we had sex last night. "No, we didn't," she says, garnering my attention.

"How did you know I was thinking that?"

Reaching up, I cup her breasts with my hands and massage them. She moans. "Because I know all your tells."

"I think I know yours too."

"And what do I want?" she breathlessly asks, as she continues to circle her hips on my cock.

"Right now, you want me to fuck you."

"Mmmhmpf," she says. Her eyes still closed as she continues to ride me.

"Then what are you waiting for?"

She opens her eyes and stares down at me. "Nothing." She lifts her hips and slides down my cock. Her walls hugging me tightly. With her eyes locked on mine, she rides me as if she's a cowgirl. Bucking, fucking, holding on like her life depends on it. And unlike a rodeo, I last for longer than eight seconds.

Together, we reach our crescendo and we shout each other's names as we bathe in orgasmic pleasure. She collapses onto my chest, "I've missed that," she mumbles into my neck.

"So you only missed me this past week for my cock?"

"Not just your cock." She lifts her head. "I've been miserable without you, Nic. I'm sorry that I didn't give you a chance to explain what I overheard. I'm sorry I eavesdropped. I'm sorry I pushed you away, but most of all, I'm sorry I didn't tell you I was pregnant sooner."

"You have nothing to apologize for. We're together now and that's all that matters, and I promise you I'll be here every step of the way, Charli. Can I come to your next appointment?"

She lifts her head. "You can come to them all." She leans forward and presses her lips to mine. What starts out as a slow and sensual kiss, quickly turns heated and carnal. Flipping Charli to her back, I line my once again hard dick up at her entrance and slide in.

Her pussy was made for my cock.

With our eyes fused to each other, we make love.

Slow and sweet love.

Charli Davis is it for me, now and forever.

After a lazy morning in bed together, we order an Uber and head back to Baylor and Corey's place to collect my bike. When Charli heard I rode over, she was excited to go for a ride. We showered separately, because if we'd showered together, I would have taken her again and I don't think my cock, or her pussy, needs another work out.

Baylor and Corey aren't home so Charli texts her to let her know we've collected my bike. Charli hops on behind me, having her pressed against me is the best feeling in the world. Not wanting to go straight home, I ask her if she's up for an adventure. She nods so I jump on to the I-94 E and head toward Michigan City.

Parking my bike, we head to a hole-in-the-wall fish and chip shop and then head to the water's edge for a midafternoon picnic.

"It's so beautiful here."

"It sure is," I tell her, my eyes locked on her and not the view.

"I meant the view."

"I know, the view from where I'm sitting is the most gorgeous view I have ever seen. Angel, you are glowing."

She looks to me and smiles. "Would you believe today is the first day that I haven't been sick since I found out?"

"Really?" I question.

"Yep, and I think it's because of you. Since seeing you yesterday afternoon and clearing the air, I've felt this weight lift. I'm not as anxious or stressed."

"Well, that's good, because anxiety and stress are not good for babies."

"And when did you become Mr. Baby-Know-It-All?"

"This morning when you were asleep after you sexually attacked me."

"I sexually attacked you?" she questions.

"Yep, I was just lying there when you straddled me and took advantage of lil' old me."

"I didn't hear you complaining."

"Not complaining, just stating that you started it."

"Keep that up and you won't get attacked ever again."

"Like you can stay away from this?" I jump up and strike a pose. Charli laughs and it's like music to my ears. Offering her my hand, I pull her up and into my arms. Sliding one around her waist, I stare into her eyes. "For what it's worth, you can sexually attack me like that anytime you want."

"Anytime, eh?"

"Yep, anytime."

"How quick can you get us back to your place?"

Throwing her over my shoulder, she squeals and laughs as I hoof it back to my bike. Slapping her ass for good measure. She moans and it goes straight to my cock.

"Did my slapping your ass just turn you on?"

"Yes, everything about you turns me on and since I've become pregnant, my sexual appetite has increased. I hope you're ready for this."

"If it means I get to fuck you twenty-four seven, then bring it on."

"Then take me home, Biker Boy, and—"

Cutting her off, I place a chaste kiss on her lips. We climb on my bike and I speed back to my place, breaking quite a few road rules, but the fines will be worth it. My girl wants to fuck and what my girl wants, my girl gets.

DARREN CHIKATILO 29

SHOULD HAVE KNOWN THAT DEAR OLD BROTHER WOULD FUCK all of this up. I told him not to get involved with Vlahos. I told him we had enough and would be fine, but no, he didn't listen and now he's in jail and our money is in limbo. And to top it off, that bitch is playing dumb. I was hoping getting her suspended would get her to falter and give me the location of the money, but she's locked up tighter than a nun's cunt. Seems she's loyal to Dean and only him, she should know that I'm the one in charge.

I'm sitting on an uncomfortable chair in the visitation area at the prison, waiting for my brother. I've had enough of this shit, I want my money and I want it now. My patience has run out and it's time for them to give me the answers I need.

Looking at my watch, I shake my head when I realize I've been waiting here for twenty minutes, he's still not here and the anger I was already harboring is getting stronger by the minute. The buzzer sounds and I look up to see Dean walking toward me, he has a black eye and a busted nose.

"The fuck happened to you?"

"Dominic Cruz."

"The partner?"

He nods. "The fucker sucker punched me when I wouldn't give him information to clear Charli's name."

"Speaking of the cunt, what are we going to do about her? She's still not complying."

"It's hard to comply when you don't know shit," he tells me, but I know that she knows something. You don't work closely with someone like those two did and not know about every aspect of each other's life—legal and illegal. Besides, he wouldn't be protecting her otherwise. I'm starting to suspect that she and my brother are conspiring against me. He better still be on my side, I don't give a rat's ass that he's family, if he's betrayed me, I will have no qualms in taking him out.

"You cannot tell me that she knows nothing. Why are you protecting her? Just get her to give up the goods and this can all be over."

"I've told you, I hadn't implemented the incrimination of her before I was incarcerated."

"So you say, I need to get this finalized. I can't hold them off any longer."

"Once I'm out of here, it will all work out."

"I can't wait that fucking long. This is all because you got involved in something I told you not to. If you'd just stuck to the original plan, I'd be free of my mess and we'd be on a beach living it up in Fiji."

"We needed him for protection, you know that."

"And look at what you ended up getting instead?"

"You need to get past this, Darren. I will be out soon

and then we can proceed with the final steps." Reaching over, he taps my cheek. "Patience, dear brother. Patience."

"My patience has run out," I growl, slamming my fist on the table. "I fucking told you not to get involved with Vlahos. I knew something would happen and what do you know, I was correct. He's dead. You're locked up, and the money is in limbo because you fucked up."

"Fuck you, asshole," he snarls. "As I've repeatedly told you, we needed the protection he could offer us."

"And I told you I had it sorted, you've ruined this for me…I mean…us."

He shakes his head and glares at me. "I will get you what you want as soon as I'm out of here. That was always the deal."

"I'll just pay the little bitch a visit, she'll give it up and then I'll work on getting you out."

"You can try but I assure you, she doesn't know what you want to know. I keep telling you that, but you aren't listening."

"Don't protect her. I will kill her and you if it have to."

"Right now, brother dearest, you need me more than I need you. Look around," he waves his hand around, "three meals a day. Roof over my head. I'm safe in here, you can't touch me. You, on the other hand, you're out there without the one thing you want. I have the power to bring you down if I so choose, but I gave you my word and I still stand by that. Now. Get me the fuck out of here and we can finish what we started."

I growl at my brother, "Don't mess with me. One call and I can end you in there." I point behind him.

"And then you'll be up shit creek without a paddle." He leans forward. "Get me the fuck out of here and then I will help you. Until that happens, my lips are sealed." He mimes zipping his lips. Rising up, Dean rests his palms on the edge of the metal table and he stares down at me. "Get me the fuck out of here, Darren." He turns on his heel, and stalks away from me, just before he steps out of sight; he looks over his shoulder. "Clocks ticking, asshole."

Slamming my fist on the table, I growl, "Fuck." Standing up, I stride out of the room, my head held high, not letting on that I'm pissed the fuck off. My blood is boiling. Signing out of the prison, I walk to my car, climb into the driver's seat, and head back to my place.

Walking inside, I flop down on the ratty sofa. I'm running out of patience. I want my money and I want it now. I need to up my game if I'm going to get this sorted quickly. It's time to up the stakes. Charli Davis is about to pay up. She needs to realize, I always get what's owed and my brother can fuck right off if he thinks I'm waiting. I wait for no one. Game on, bitch!

CHARLI 30

Waking in Nic's arms is fast becoming my favorite way to wake up. But it comes a close second to his head between my thighs. The pregnancy sex hormones are running rampant through me at the moment. Lately, each and every time I look at Nic, my panties dampen and I have to jump him. My sexual need has gotten so out of control that he bought me a rabbit to give his cock a break. And I have to say, using 'Ronnie the Rabbit' while he's watching me is such a turn-on that usually after I've given myself a self-induced orgasm, he gives me a Nic-induced one too. Hashtag winning.

"Morning, Angel," he says, in his deep and gruff voice. It sends shivers through me and I shudder in his arms. "Did you just come from me saying good morning?"

"No," I smack his chest and giggle, lifting my head up, I gaze into his baby blues, "but my panties are now soaked."

"You're not wearing any," he whispers as he rolls on top of me, cocooning me under him.

"Are you complaining?" Raising my eyebrows suggestively at him, I spread my legs and lift my hips, rubbing myself on his morning wood. His cock hardens further between us. Grabbing my arms, he raises them up, pressing them into the mattress as he begins to slide the tip of his dick up and down my slit. His eyes are locked on mine when he presses his length inside of me.

"Nic," I moan, as my body adjusts to his girth. He thrusts in and out of me, ever so slowly. "Faster," I mewl, scratching my nails down his back. He presses his lips to mine and kisses me deeply. Our tongues slide back and forth in sync with his dick down below.

Breaking the kiss, he stares down at me and lifts my leg over his shoulder. Hitting that magical spot with each thrust of his hips. "Niiiiiiic," I scream as my orgasm explodes. My body coming alive from head to toe as pleasure courses through me.

Nic's body tenses and he grunts through his release, "Fuck, I love you."

"I love you too," I pant, as he lowers my leg and collapses to the mattress next to me.

Rolling to my side, I snuggle into him. "What do you think of the name Carter if it's a girl."

"Carter Davis, I like it."

"No, Cruz. She, or he, will have your last name."

"Are you sure?"

"Yep, because hopefully one day, I'll have that last name too."

"Charli Cruz, I like that just as much as Carter Cruz."

"And if it's a boy DJ, Dominic Junior."

"I don't hate that either."

"Then it's sorted, Carter for a girl and DJ for a boy."

With a smile on my face, I lie here and enjoy the moment, not knowing that in the coming weeks, my bliss bubble will be popped when everything unravels.

CHARLI 31

...ten weeks later

I'M SITTING OUT ON NIC'S DECK, ENJOYING A CHEESEBURGER and biding time 'til my doctor's appointment later this afternoon. The joys of being on suspension for something that you didn't do, time, lots of time on my hands. Nic is going to meet me there and we will get to see our baby and maybe find out the sex. I think I want a surprise, there are very few surprises in life but Nic, along with Bay, want to find out.

My phone rings, halting my decision/thoughts on finding out the sex. Looking down, I scrunch face up when I see it's Patrick from IA calling me. I know he's just doing his job but he doesn't help the stigma given to Internal Affairs agents, he really is a power hungry asshole.

"This is Charli," I say as I answer.

"I need you to come into the office," he says, no greeting or pleasantries.

"I'm sorry, who is this?" If he wants to be a dick I can be one too.

"It's Patrick from IA," he snaps.

"Hi, Patrick," I say, stalling, and wanting to piss him off. "How are you today? I'm great, thanks for asking."

"I need you to come into the office, now."

"I'm sorry, Patrick, I have a doctor's appointment, I can come in after that."

"I said now," he shouts down the line.

"And I said, I'll be there after my doctor's appointment. See you later."

Not giving him a chance to reply, I hang up and throw my phone down next to me. "Asshole," I growl, as I take a big bite of my cheeseburger.

⎯◯◯⎯

Nic and I walk back into the office hand in hand, he's still gripping tightly to the sonogram picture of our little girl, showing anyone and everyone the picture of our lil' munchkin. I decided yes, in a spur of the moment decision when the doctor asked if we wanted to know the sex, I wanted to know.

Our elation soon dissipates when we step into the office and are met with a scowling Patrick from IA. "Follow me, Agent Davis," he growls, turning on his heel and walking toward the conference room.

"Do you want me to come with you?" Nic asks me.

Shaking my head, I smile, "Nah," watching him walk away, I add, "I have nothing to hide, I'll be fine." I follow him to the conference room and wonder how can someone be so unpeopley? I used to feel sorry for Patrick and the IA guys but after this, nope, not at all. They are power hungry dicks, plain and simple.

Before I've sat down, Patrick cuts to it. "Charli Davis, you are officially terminated from the FBI."

"Come again?" I ask him. "Did you just say I've been terminated?" Clearly, I heard wrong just now.

"Yes, I did." He growls at having to repeat himself. "You no longer are an employee here. We have found the smoking gun I need to bring your deceptive lying ass down. Did you think I would not discover that you've been laundering money?"

"What evidence?" I ask.

"You've been laundering money that links back to Vlahos, Ciccone, and several other illegal operations that we have been investigating."

"Whatever you have is fake," I tell him again. "I'm innocent," I protest but from the stern look on his face, he doesn't believe me.

"That's what they all say." He pompously stands up and glares down at me. "I suggest you find yourself a good lawyer because with what I have on you, you'll be joining Dean behind bars very soon, and if I have it my way, the two of you will be going away for a very long time."

"But—"

"No buts, Davis, you're out." He picks up his file and smugly adds, "Better get used to the color orange."

He walks out of the conference room leaving me stunned, alone, and jobless. A hand touches my shoulder, startling me. Lifting my head up, I see Nic staring down at me. Concern etched on his gorgeous face. "What happened?" he asks, his voice laced with apprehension and worry.

"I…I've been terminated."

"What?" he growls, "This is horseshit."

Nodding my head, I begin to cry. "Nic," I wail, "Our baby is going to be born in jail. I'm a shit mom before she's even taken a breath."

"No!" He drops to his knees in front of me and grips my hands in his. "Our baby will not be born in prison. I will figure this out…somehow. I won't let that happen."

"How?" I cry. "He seems pretty confident that what he has will stick and I'll be sharing a cell with Dean."

"I don't know how yet but, Angel, I promise. I will not let you down."

Resting my head on his shoulder, I continue to cry and think how I'm going to get out of this, but before I can think, Patrick the IA jackass—his new name—returns.

"You need to leave the premises, Davis, you are no longer an employee of the FBI."

"I'm her partner, she's here visiting me."

"She's a known criminal, Agent Cruz, and is no longer allowed, or welcome, in the building."

"You—" Nic goes to berate Patrick, the IA jackass, when I interrupt, "It's fine, I was just leaving."

Turning to Nic, I cup his cheek. "I'll see you at your place later." Lifting to my toes, I place a kiss on his lips. Picking up my bag, I exit the conference room and when I step out, I feel everyone watching me as walk toward the elevator.

"Charli," Bec says just as the door opens, "I will fix this."

"You sound like Nic," I tell her and sadly smile.

"Well, then listen to us, he and I will fix this."

Nodding, the doors close and the metal car takes me down to the parking lot. Walking over to my car, I climb in and before I head home, I make a stop to visit Dean.

Going through the check-in procedure, I wait in the visiting room. He walks toward me, looking confused to see me.

"What are you doing here?" he asks me.

"Like you don't know," I snarkily say.

"Has something happened?"

"You could say that. I've been fired because apparently you and I have been laundering money together." His eyes widen when I say this. "Is that why you were working with Vlahos? To launder money?" He stares blankly at me. "Why are you doing this to me, Dean? I was nothing but a good partner and friend to you, and this is how you repay me." My eyes well with tears, "Why, Dean? Why?" My hand drops to my belly, I lift my gaze and plead. "I'm pregnant, Dean." His breath hitches and his eyes widen at this revelation. "The stress of this isn't good for me, or the baby." I pause, wiping away a stray tear. I take a deep breath, "Be the man I know you are, Dean. Deep down you're a good guy, you've just lost your way. Don't let what you and your brother have gotten yourselves into affect me anymore. Own your mistakes and do the right thing, please. It's not just my life at stake anymore."

Standing up, I turn and walk away. Before I exit, I look over my shoulder. "Do the right thing, Dean," I tell him before I push the door open and walk away from him. I have no idea if my plea will make a difference or if it all just fell on deaf ears. I hope with everything I have that I got through to him.

Looking back through the glass, I see him still sitting there, staring into space. He's processing my words and I have a feeling he's going to do the right thing, well I hope he is.

Stepping outside, I walk down the stairs and turn toward the parking lot and take a deep breath. I hate the smell of the prison. I need to go home and have a shower and wash off all the icky prison stench. Then I'm going to laze on the sofa, order McDonald's delivery—again—and eat all the cheeseburgers. Once my tummy is full, I'm going to crawl into bed, sleep like Sleeping Beauty and then tomorrow, I'll come up with a plan to end all this.

That feeling of being watched has the hairs on the back of my neck standing on end. Looking around the open parking lot, I see that I'm the only one here. Shaking off the feeling, I climb into my car and head toward home but a few miles down the road, I see a McDonald's and decide to stop in for a cheeseburger...or four. At this rate, our little girl is going to come out looking like the Hamburglar.

Pulling in, the lineup for drive-through is massive and I'm in no mood to wait so I park my car and head inside. Ordering four cheeseburgers and a Sprite, garnering a Judgey McJudgerson look from the cashier, I pay for my order that could easily feed two, and technically I am two, so screw her and her Judgey McJudgerson face. With my receipt in hand, I smile politely and step aside to wait for my food.

Living up to its 'fast food' name, my order is called quickly.

Smiling at the cashier, who is still judging me, I grab my food and drink and head back to my car. Reaching into the bag, I pull out one of the delicious burgers and take a bite. Closing my eyes, I moan in delight as the greasy burger fires up my taste buds. Resting my drink on the roof my car, I dig in my bag for my keys. I'm so engrossed in looking for my keys, that I don't hear someone sneak up behind me. Before I register what's happening, everything goes dark for me and munchkin.

DEAN CHIKATILO 32

WITH CHARLI BEING PREGNANT, THIS CHANGES EVERYTHING. I was willing to bring her down to save my ass, but now that it's more than her at stake, I don't think I can do that to her. I knew using her as my scapegoat was going to bite me in the ass, but desperate times call for desperate measures. As the days go by, Darren is becoming unhinged and if he unravels any further, this will all turn to shit, well, a bigger pile of shit than it already is. Maybe it's time I fess up to everything, but I haven't come this far to lose now. I need a new plan that clears Charli but still keeps my hands clean…ish.

"Phone call, Chikatilo," the guard growls at me from outside my cell.

Nodding at him, I rise to my feet and walk over to the wall of phones. Picking up the receiver, I answer, "Hello,"

"It's happening," Darren bellows down the line. The tone and shake of his voice unnerves me. He's teetering on the edge right now and I need to be careful how I proceed from here.

"No!" I growl, "I say when it happens. You need to back off of Charli. Things have changed, she's—"

"—pregnant, I know. We need to wrap this up before she goes into labor. I want what you promised me. I've got this, Baby Brother. You will soon be free. We will have the cash. Just trust me, everything is in motion."

"What do you mean everything is in motion?"

"I'm doing what I should have done as soon as you were arrested, I'm taking control of this operation."

"But—"

"But nothing, this is happening, Dean, and there's nothing you can say or do to stop it."

He hangs up and I mumble, "Shit. Fuck. Shit." I stare at the wall, Charli is in danger and it's all my fault. This is turning into a raging inferno. I need to act now if I'm going to protect what's mine, as well as Charli and her unborn baby.

Picking up the receiver again, I dial the one person who I know will help me.

"Dean?" a shy timid voice says after accepting the call.

"Yeah, baby, it's me."

"What's wrong?" she questions.

"Darren is going to do something and I need to try to stop it because things have changed."

"What's changed?" she asks.

"Charli is pregnant."

"Wow, that certainly wasn't expected."

"I know, kinda throws a wrench in the works, and with Darren becoming more and more unhinged, I need you to stop him from doing something stupid."

"I'll do what I can, baby." The line goes quiet, and then

Lana quietly says, "I think I did something wrong that may have added to Darren's mood."

My gut churns. "Lana, baby, what did you do?"

"A while ago, I sent a message to that agent you mentioned, Cruz. Hoping to throw the focus on to Darren because I know deep down you don't want to hurt Charli. The Cruz guy, well he came here. I ummm, ahh, I gave him hints without incriminating us or anything. And Darren, umm, knows he was here. I'm sorry, I didn't mean to lie to you but I just want you home. I miss you. I thought if I cleared your name, you'd be out."

"Yes, it was stupid, but I've been feeling the same." Closing my eyes, I rub my forehead and sigh, "Baby, it'll be fine. I'm…I'm thinking of coming clean. Darren is losing it and I don't know how much longer I can keep up this charade. Now with Charli—"

"Darren was ranting and raving about her while he was here. Saying she knows but is being a c-word about it all, and it's time for him to make her pay. Does he mean what I think he means?"

"If you think he means taking her and getting the info he wants then yes, you are thinking like him." I pause. "Baby, I need you to do me a favor."

"Anything," she says, and I know she means it. She may play the dumb bimbo but underneath that facade is a kick-ass woman who I'm crazy about.

"I need you to get in touch with Cruz again and this time, I need you to tell him everything."

"Everything?" she repeats, her voice laced with concern, but the time to confess all is now.

"No, don't tell him everything, everything, but enough to get him intrigued and then you need to convince him to come and see me."

"Are you sure about this?"

"No, but this has gone on long enough and it needs to end."

"Will you be safe?"

"I'll be fine, baby." *I'm not one-hundred percent sure.* "But it's Charli I have concerns for now. She doesn't deserve Darren's wrath for my lies and deceit."

"Will Darren kill us?" she fearfully asks.

"Us? No. Charli? Possibly, but this is a risk we have to take. I can't let an innocent woman and her unborn baby take the fall for my mess. I never should have involved her, but desperate times—"

"—called for desperate measures. I know, baby. I don't like this but I will do everything you've asked." She pauses. "I love you and I'm so proud of you. Sure, this hasn't quite gone to plan but together, you and I can conquer anything thrown our way."

"I love you too, baby, but whatever you do, do not—I repeat—do not, let on to Darren that we're going to flip on him. He will kill you in the blink of an eye and I can't lose you."

"I promise, Dean. My lips are sealed when it comes to your crazy brother."

We say our goodbyes and hang up.

Walking back to my cell, I hope with everything I have that Lana can get in touch with Dominic and keep Charli safe, but I know my brother, he will stop at nothing to get his money. He'd even kill a pregnant woman who, like Jon Snow, knows nothing.

DOMINIC 33

WATCHING CHARLI LEAVE RIGHT NOW WAS HARD. I WANTED to smash Patrick from IA in the face but I know that won't help Charli, or me. Turning on my heel, I walk into Amanda's office, slamming the door behind me. She looks up and purses her lips at me. "This is horseshit," I snarl, dropping into the seat before her.

"I agree," she says, leaning forward she rests her elbows on her desk and her chin in her fingertips. "What are you suggesting we do?"

"Clear Charli's name."

She nods. "And how do you propose we do that?"

"I was hoping you'd have an idea because I have nothing right now. What's this so called evidence they have?"

"They haven't disclosed that to me."

"This is horseshit," I scoff, again. Staring at the floor, I lean forward and rest my elbows on my knees and cradle my head. I let out a frustrated sigh.

"So you've said. Twice now." Lifting my head, I stare across the desk at her.

"Well, it is," I say like a petulant child.

"Cruz, I want you to go home and be with Charli this afternoon. She will need you, even though she'll be stubborn and pretend like she doesn't." I nod and grin at this because that's exactly what my Angel is like. "We can meet again tomorrow morning with a fresh and horseshit-free head. Then we'll come up with a game plan to fix this mess."

Nodding in agreement, I agree, "I like this new plan. I'll see you bright and early in the morning."

Tapping her desk, I stand up and exit her office. I head back to mine to grab my things and just as I enter my desk phone rings. I contemplate ignoring it but something compels me to answer. "Cruz," I say in greeting.

"This is Lana."

"Lana," I repeat, the name sounds familiar but I can't quite place it right now.

"From Manhattan Vaults."

"Yes, Lana, how can I help you today?"

"I…umm…ahh, Dean—"

"What about the asshole?"

"He's not an asshole. He asked me to call you and warn you."

"Warn me about what?"

"Darren."

"What about Darren?"

"He's going to do something stupid if you don't get to him first."

"What's he going to do?" But as I ask the question, I think I already know what she's going to say.

"He's sick of waiting and he's going to go after Charli. He...he's going to plant evidence—"

"You're a bit late with the warning, that's already happened."

"Ohh," she says, "I'm booked on a flight later tonight, can I meet with you?"

"Why do you want to meet with me?"

The line is silent for a moment and then she says, "I'll tell you everything when I get there."

"Why are you helping me now? Why the change of heart? When I came to see you, you were locked up as tight as your vaults."

"Dean doesn't want anything to happen to Charli, now that he knows she's pregnant."

"How does he know she's pregnant?" I ask.

"He didn't say but now that she is, it changes things. Can I meet with you tomorrow?"

"What times does your flight get in?"

"Around six, as long as Delta is on time."

"Come straight to my office, I can't wait 'til tomorrow to see you."

"Okay, I'll see you later, Agent Cruz."

Hanging up from her, I grab my phone to call Charli and give her the good news. It goes to voicemail. "Hey, baby, it's me. I'll be home later than I hoped but I think I have something that will clear your name. Love you."

Standing up, I walk back to Amanda's office and fill her in on the call with Lana just now. "That's great news," she says. "I'd like to be here when you meet with Lana too."

"Of course," I tell her.

Heading back to my office, I sit down at my computer and try and concentrate but my mind can't focus. I keep looking at the clock, I swear time is actually ticking slower. My phone pings with a text and I see it's from Abi.

ABI: *Check this out, I'm getting it for baby Cruz **link attached***

It's a website that makes baby clothing and Abi's getting a onesie that says, "A U N T I E, I'll be there for you." In a *Friends* layout. I laugh and shake my head.

NIC: *Love it. So will our little girl*

No sooner do I hit send, my phone rings in my hand. Swiping, I answer but before I can say anything, she screams, "It's a girl!"

"Yep," I confirm, grinning that I will have a little girl in a few months' time. "We found out this morning."

"And why am I only finding out now?"

"Because I have work and the world does not revolve around you, Abs."

"A text would have sufficed." Then she adds, "Mom is gonna flip her shit when she finds out she's getting a granddaughter."

"Umm, how about Dad? He's more gaga for this baby than Mom is."

"This is true," she agrees. "This lil' princess is going to be spoiled rotten but she will love her Aunty Abs the most."

"Don't let Elena hear you say that."

"Pffft, like she stands a chance against me." Shaking my head, I just laugh. "Anyway, Aunty Abs has to go. Give Charli's belly a kiss for me and punch yourself in the face."

Before I can reply, she hangs up. Throwing my phone onto my desk, I bring up the website Abi sent me on my desktop. I start looking at the site and when I see a pink onesie with "Daddy's Little FBI Agent" on it, I order one straightaway.

After completing the transaction, I call Charli again, but again it goes to voicemail. Worry seeps in but if I know her, she will be curled up on the couch with a cheeseburger, or three, and will be engrossed in reruns of *One Tree Hill*.

A knock at my door garners my attention, and when I look up I see Amanda and Lana standing there. "Hey," I say to them both, as I stand up and round my desk. "Should we talk in here or in the conference room?"

"Conference room," Amanda says, she turns, and walks away. Silently Lana and I follow her. Closing the door behind me, I walk to the other side of the table and take a seat across from Lana and Amanda.

"Okay, Lana," Amanda says, "Dominic tells me you have information that may help Charli."

She nods her head, "Earlier today, I got a call from Dean—"

"What's your relationship with him?" Amanda asks her.

"He and I have been seeing each other for just over twelve months now. We met when he and his brother came into Manhattan Vaults."

"And why did they need your services?" Amanda asks her. This is the first time I've seen Boss Lady in agent action and she's a no-holds-barred agent. She's totally badass and I can see why she's the boss around here.

"At the beginning, I had no idea of what they were up to, but as Dean and I got closer, my role changed. I started to accept the deliveries. Darren wasn't too impressed that I was assisting them. Darren likes to think he's the boss but he's dumb as dogshit."

"Okay, how does Charli and Vlahos fit into this?"

"Dean wanted protection and he thought Vlahos was the answer. During the setup with Vlahos taking over the security, he was arrested and all assets that Dean had fronted were seized. As fate would have it, Dean was assigned to watch the witness girlfriend chick and the agent. Vlahos went off track and wanted revenge, he wasn't impressed with being screwed over by his supposed queen. Dean managed to locate the frozen assets and retrieved them from evidence, using Charli as his scapegoat. All evidence against her is fabricated by Darren, Dean, and me. The IA guy investigating Charli is in Dean's pocket too."

"That fucking asshole," I growl, slamming my fist on the table. "I knew Patrick was a cocksucker."

"Cruz," Amanda warns me. She turns her attention back to Lana. "You're telling me that Patrick Fitzpatrick is working with Dean?"

She nods her head. "You'd be surprised how money can sway people."

"So why are you telling us this now?"

"Dean is worried that Darren is losing control and now that Charli is pregnant, he doesn't want her to stress over this and cause harm to the baby."

"So if she wasn't pregnant, he'd still be letting her take the fall?" I question her.

She shrugs at me. "How do we know that this isn't just another ploy? For all we know, you could be throwing Patrick under the bus too?"

"Why would I incriminate myself with more lies?" She has a point but I'm still not convinced.

"Will you be willing to testify to this?" Amanda asks her.

She nods. "Yes, I'm willing but I would like to make a deal for myself and Dean."

"For you, that's possible. For him? Not a chance in hell."

Excusing myself, I step out of the room and dial Charli's number but this time it goes straight to voicemail. I can't wait to tell her the good news, but I will be here with Amanda for the next few hours getting this all documented. It's too late to visit Dean tonight to get him to corroborate Lana's story, but my gut is telling me it's the truth.

Walking back into the interrogation room, I feel lighter. I can't believe that this time tomorrow it will all be over. Charli is going to be so relieved to be free of these accusations.

CHARLI 34

Opening my eyes, everything around me is fuzzy. The last thing I remember is eating a cheeseburger on the way to my car and then nothing. Blinking a few times, the room comes into focus and my heart rate increases as I glance around. I'm in a basement, the walls are cement and covered in grime. In the center of the room is a set of rickety-looking stairs that head upstairs. From the dim light coming from a single bulb above me, I continue to look around and apart from the chair I'm tied to, the room is pretty bare. There's a busted water heater in a corner and a few boxes scattered throughout. There's a musty smell in the air from there being no windows and it's a little on the chilly side down here.

I've never seen this place before and I have no idea where I am. Panic begins to fester but I know for the sake of munchkin, and me, I need to remain calm. Closing my eyes, I take a few deep breaths but it has the opposite effect on me and I vomit. Turning my head to the side, I empty my stomach on myself and the floor—now the rooms smells musty and vomity.

The door at the top of the stairs slams open and I hear feet stomp down the stairs, looking up my mouth drops open when I see Darren Chikatilo walking toward me.

"You're finally awake," he teases, but the playful look on his face drops when he sees the vomit on the floor and all over me. "Ugh, you dirty fucking bitch," he snarls, the playful look is gone and it's replaced with disgust. "Why'd you vomit?" He stands there staring at me, waiting for me to answer him. "I asked you a fucking question, why did you fucking vomit?"

"The smell down here didn't agree with me."

"Tough fucking shit. Do not vomit again."

We stare at one another, the air thickening with disdain for one another. My stomach rumbles, breaking the silence and then I remember I was at McDonald's when he took me, "Where are my cheeseburgers?"

"What?" he snaps

"My cheeseburgers and Sprite, where are they?" From the look on his face, my burgers and drink are not here and he doesn't give a rat's ass about them. "Think you can get me some more?" I ask, hoping that if I keep him occupied, I can find a way out of here, but unless I become Houdini, I'll be stuck to this chair for the foreseeable future.

"Fuck you and fuck your cheeseburgers. Gimme what's mine and then you can have all the fucking cheeseburgers you like."

"I can't think on an empty stomach," I sass back. His face morphs from nothing to anger in the blink of an eye. This guy is seriously unhinged and I need to stop taunting him. My burgers will have to wait but as soon as I get out of here, I will be eating my weight in the cheesy greasy burgers.

He storms over to me and rests his palms on my thighs, digging his fingers in painfully. For a scrawny guy, he sure has some strength. I wince in pain as his nails dig farther in, thankful to be wearing linen pants to prevent him from breaking the skin but I will surely be bruised. "Give me my fucking money!" he yells in my face, spittle and his foul heated breath hits my skin, causing my stomach to roll again. I can feel the lump building in the back of my throat, I'm going to vomit any second. If he was pissed before at me hurling, he'll really be pissed if I vomit on him.

Lady Luck is on my side because he pushes himself back, letting me breathe. The dank basement smell isn't much better but at least the need to vomit has disappeared, ish.

"This will be home until I get what's mine." He stares at me. "Give me what I'm owed and then you can breathe some fresh fucking air."

"I really don't know what it is you want, Darren."

"Don't fucking lie to me. You, Dean, and his lil' bitch are conspiring to cut me out. I just know it."

"Cut you out of what?"

"Shut up," he growls, stepping toward me he slaps my cheek. My head snaps to the side from the force. Copper fills my mouth. The taste of the blood causes the need to vomit to reappear and before I can stop myself, I vomit all over myself. It comes up so quickly that I don't have time to turn my head and I vomit down the front of me.

"Ugh, really?" He turns his back on me and storms back upstairs, slamming the door shut behind him.

My eyes well with tears. Closing my eyes, I take a few

deep breaths, the feeling to vomit is still there and increasing with each breath. The smell down here really isn't agreeing with me. Taking a few more deep breaths, I calm my racing heart but it doesn't do much to ease the ill feeling building in my stomach. Opening my eyes, I stare at a spot on the wall and try to calm myself down, I cannot let fear take over right now. I need to remain strong, for me and munchkin. That determination is the only thing keeping me going right now, I will not let this asshole win.

The door above flies open, slamming into the wall again. Turning my head, I watch as dust and dirt particles flutter in the air. Darren marches back down the stairs with my handbag, my phone is in his hand. He walks over and stops in front of me. "Passcode" he growls. Waving my phone in my face, I stare at him blankly. "Passcode," he snarls through clenched teeth. "Your phone is going off so we need to text lover boy so he doesn't come looking for you."

"Where is here?" I ask, hoping he'll give me something to work with, but I don't think he's that dumb.

He ignores my question. "Passcode!"

"465702," I tell him, he punches the code in, and smirks. "Seems lover boy misses you, there's a few voice-mails and texts."

He begins to type a message and reads as he types.

CHARLI: *Need space. Today has been hell. I'll be in touch when I'm ready.*

"That should keep the asshole at bay." He presses send and stares at my phone in his hand, his eyes widen. Nic must be typing back. "Ohh look, a reply." He reads it to me.

NIC: *Please don't push me away, Angel. We will fix this, I have something that may clear you. Just remember I love you. I'll see you tomorrow XoXoX*

"Aww, he thinks he can clear you and that he'll see you tomorrow. How sweet...and naïve." He looks at me with a sinister grin. "He might be able to clear your name but see you tomorrow, well that's entirely up to you." Without saying another word, he walks back upstairs and turns the lone light off, leaving me in darkness.

The basement is eerie and scarier in the dark.

I can hear him stomping around upstairs and then it's silent. As the saying goes, 'silence is deafening.' I can't handle the silence anymore so I start to sing to myself. First I start with my mantra song, "Stronger" by Britney, which morphs into "Fighter' by Christina Aguilera. I'm belting out "Sweet Home Alabama" by Lynyrd Skynyrd when the door above flies opens.

"Shut the fuck up!" Darren shouts down the stairs, slamming the door shut once again.

Not wanting to anger him further, I close my eyes, hoping to get some sleep. Exhaustion takes over and I drift off to sleep, but I'm rudely woken the next morning when Darren throws freezing cold water on me. "Shit," I mutter as the cool water trickles down my arms and front.

"You going to tell me what I want to know?" he asks, leaning against the wall, he crosses his arms over his chest and he stares at me.

I shrug. "I don't know what you want."

"You know what I want," he growls.

Shaking my head side to side, I stare up at him. "I don't, Darren. I really have no clue what it is you think I have. I wish I knew because I would give it to you in a heartbeat if I did."

Clearly my answer isn't what he wants because he storms toward me, pulls his hand back, and slaps me hard across the face, repeatedly. My head flopping side to side from the slaps. His motion become wilder and faster. The chair begins to rock from the force, I feel like I'm going to topple over but at the last minute, he viciously grips me by shoulders and steadies me. Digging his fingers roughly into my arms.

"You will tell me," he snarls before walking away. He spins on his heel, lifts his hands, and laces his fingers, bringing them to the back of his head. Flexing his arms, he glares at me. "Where's my fucking money?"

"I don't know," I tell him, again.

"Don't lie to me!" he shouts, the tone in his voice unnerving. He's starting to lose control, I need to placate him, who knows what he'll do next. "Dean said you didn't know but I know the two of you are conspiring to cut me out. He's a cunt. You're a cunt. You're all cunts who think they can pull the wool over my eyes. I refuse to be cut—"

"Cut you out of what?" I interrupt, "Darren, listen to me, I really," I place emphasis on the word really, "don't know what you're talking about."

"Bullshit," he scoffs, gripping my upper arms again, he stares into my eyes. His pupils are dilated. His face is full of anger and rage. I know no matter what I say, it will fall on deaf ears. "I will get what's mine and I don't care if I have to kill you, him, and anyone who gets in my way." He shoves me away from him and the chair topples backward. I land with a thud. My head bouncing on the cement. Both of my arms are pinned under the chair, I scream out in pain at being trapped. He stares down at me manically laughing, it reminds of a witch's cackle. He shakes his head and walks away from me, leaving me trapped.

Wriggling around, I eventually manage to get my left arm free but my right is pinned and from the angle I'm currently lying in, I'm pretty sure my shoulder is dislocated. With everything I have I roll, wriggle, and rock. Trying to free my pinned arm but nothing works. I'm halted in my efforts when a searing pain tears through my shoulder, yep, it's dislocated. I try again but I can't free myself and each time I move the pain increases.

Not giving up, I try one last time but this time, a pain worse than what I just experienced with my shoulder begins low in my stomach. Breathing through clenched teeth, my eyes widen when a piercing stabbing pain rips through my abdomen from front to back, followed by a warm wetness between my thighs. My eyes widen and I freeze, when I look down, I see my linen pants are stained with blood, the patch getting bigger before my eyes. "Noooo," I cry. I try and wriggle free but each time I move that pain in my shoulder and belly intensifies. Through my tears, I whimper, "I'm losing my baby."

DOMINIC 35

LEAVING THE PRECINCT, I HEAD TO MY PLACE BUT WHEN I arrive home, I find it's empty. I try calling Charli but once again, it rings out, sending me to voicemail. Jumping onto my bike since it's faster, I head over to her place but when I let myself in, I find it empty too.

Dropping to her sofa, I lean back and sigh. My phone pings with a text, I smile when I see it's from her.

CHARLI: *Need space. Today has been hell. I'll be in touch when I'm ready.*

Her words hurt, I get wanting to be alone but I want to be there for her. Even if it's just to hold her while she cries, plus I have news that will surely cheer her up. Guessing that she's at Bay's, I decide I'll give her tonight but tomorrow, tomorrow she will talk to me and I will tell her no more blocking me out. We are in this together and I want to be there to help her when times are tough, not just when they're good. I've never felt like this about anyone before and now that I have her, I'm not letting her go. She can push me away but I will always push back, always.

I send her a text reconfirming all of this.

NIC: *Please don't push me away, Angel. We will fix this, I have something that may clear you. Just remember I love you. I'll see you tomorrow XoXoX*

Standing up from her couch, I lock up and head back to my place. Falling into bed, sleep doesn't come easy because I'm worried about Charli. Eventually I drift off but I wake with a start just as the sun is rising, a feeling of unease washes over me.

I know it's early but my need to see Charli is strong, so I grab my things and head into the garage. Normally I'd take my bike but it's raining so it looks like I'll be driving and not riding today. I stop at McDonald's and grab four coffees and four cheeseburgers. Knowing that these will be what my girl wants/needs.

With the coffees and food on the passenger seat, I drive over to Baylor and Corey's place. My face scrunches when I don't see her car out front. "Maybe she's on the side street," I whisper, as I grab the drinks and burgers. Ringing the doorbell I wait, nerves flutter in my stomach the longer I wait. Pressing the doorbell again, the door finally swings open and I'm met with a sleepy scowling Baylor. "Is there any reason you're on my doorstep at stupid o'clock, Cruz?"

"I need to see Charli."

"So why are you here?"

"She's not here?" I question.

"No, why would she be here?" Bay asks. "Did you do

something stupid again?" She notices the coffees and helps herself to one.

"What's going on, Bay?" Corey asks, a towel around his hips. His eyes widen when he sees me in the doorway. "Cruz, what are you doing here?"

"He's looking for Charli 'cause he obviously did something stupid again," she says, taking a sip of the coffee she stole and from her sass and snark just now, I hope she burns her tongue, or chokes, or both. "He's going all out with coffee and I presume cheeseburgers, since we have coffee from McDonald's."

"I haven't done anything but after yesterday, she said she needed space so I presumed she was here with you."

"What happened yesterday?" Baylor and Corey ask in unison.

"She was fired. Dean and Darren planted fake evidence."

"That dude seriously needs to be dick punched," Baylor says, "But she's not here. Did you try her place?"

I nod and the sinking feeling that woke me earlier comes back with a vengeance. "Well, if she's not here, where is she?" I ask them, but they both shrug.

Without saying anything, I turn around and stalk to my car and head into the office, that's the only other place I think she'd be. Since it's early, traffic is light and I arrive quickly. Looking around the parking garage, I don't see her car. Picking up the coffee and burgers, I head up to our floor. It's empty when I step out of the elevator; this place is eerie when no one's here. I walk over to Charli's office but when I push the door open, a brown packing box sits on her desk. My heart hurts when I see that, but it doesn't last long because I know today we will have the evidence in hand to prove Charli is innocent and then she can get back to work.

Dejectedly, I walk to my office. Grabbing my phone, I pull up Charli's number and I hit dial. Once again it rings out. Throwing my phone onto my desk with more force than I intended, it slides across the top and bounces onto the floor. "What did that phone ever do to you?" Bec asks as she bends down, picks it up, and hands it back to me.

"Charli is missing."

"What?"

"She left here yesterday and now I can't find her."

"You don't think Dean and Darren did something? I know the girlfriend confessed to all last night, but can we really trust what she's saying?" I shrug. "I think you need to go pay Dean a visit."

Nodding, I grab my keys and head toward the elevator. The car arrives and I step in, Bec and Amanda follow. "We're coming too," Amanda says. "I heard what you told Bec. It's not like Charli to disappear like this and Bec is right, until Dean confirms what Lana said, we have to presume it was all ruse to throw us off track."

Silently we exit the elevator. We walk over to my car and climb in. Twelve minutes later, we arrive at the prison. I may have broken a few road rules to get here, but Charli is totally worth the fines. It's still early and the guards are less than impressed with our surprise morning visit, but fuck them, my girl is missing.

After what feels like an eternity, Dean is escorted into the interrogation room. "Good morning," he cheerily says, his demeanor of nonchalance pissing me off.

I snap. "Where is she?" I snarl. Grabbing him by the collar, I throw him up again the wall and press my forearm across his chest. I stare into his eyes waiting for him to answer.

"Where's who?" he asks.

"Charli, where the fuck is she?"

He shrugs. "Beats me, you should keep better track of your baby momma."

Pulling my fist back, I slam it into his face. A loud crunch echoes through the room and blood sprays all over me. "Fuck, my nose," he cries.

"Cruz," Amanda warns, "step back from the asshole. If you beat him to a pulp we won't be able to find Charli." She turns her attention to Dean. "Take a seat, Chikatilo, you and I need to have a chat and you will not lie or deceive me. Understood?"

"Yes, Boss Lady," he says, as he shoves past me and takes a seat across from Amanda.

"Call me that again and I will let him," she flicks a finger toward me, "have at you again. Now, your little girl-friend paid us a visit last night. Is everything she said true?"

He nods. "Yes, it's all true."

"Why should we believe you? You've had months to confess."

"Desperate times. Desperate measures."

"You were so desperate that you threw your partner of four years under the bus and then blackmailed the IA agent investigating your mess?"

"Desper—"

"No," Amanda emphasizes, "that's a cop-out and you know it. Charli is one of the best agents we've ever had, as were you. She was your friend and of all people you know, she doesn't deserve this. Now, where is she?"

"I don't know where she is, honestly," he tells Amanda, and from the tone and sincerity in his voice, I think he's telling the truth. "But I'll go out on a limb here and say that Darren has her. He called me yesterday and threatened he was going after her. I told him to hold off, hoping that Lana would confess all to you then she and Charli would be safe, but seems my dear old brother decided to go against my wishes."

"Where would he take her?" Bec asks. I completely forgot that she came with us.

Dean shrugs. "I don't know. You could try his place but I don't think he'd be stupid enough to go there."

"Fuck," I growl, raking my hands though my hair when it hits me. "Her phone."

"What about it?" Amanda asks.

"Charli texted me which means it's still on and it rang out to voicemail earlier this morning, we can get IT to trace it."

Before anyone can argue or agree, I turn on my heel and race out of the room, heading back to my car. Pulling my phone out while I wait for the elevator down, I dial Kat, our tech guru. "What up, Cruz?" she answers on the first ring.

"I need you to trace a cell ASAP."

"I love when you go all super secure agent suave on me, what's the number?"

"It's Charli," I say.

"Baby momma Charli?"

"Yep," I reply, letting the 'P' pop.

"Okay, leave it with me and I'll send you the coordinates of the last location as soon as I have them," she tells me.

"You're a rock star," I tell her.

"I know, find our baby momma and let me know if I can do anything else to help."

"Roger that," I tell her and disconnect the call. I climb into the driver's seat and I look over to see Amanda and Bec racing toward my car. Amanda opens the passenger door, just as my phone pings with a text from Kat. "I've got her location."

"Give it to me and I'll call for backup," Amanda says, as she takes her seat and the phone from me, she gets to arranging backup. Glancing in the rearview mirror as I back out of my spot, I see that Bec has her phone to her ear, no doubt arranging medical for my girl.

Pressing my foot down, I haul ass out of the parking lot and head to the location that Kat sent me a few moments ago. Pulling into the morning gridlock, I slam the steering wheel in frustration. "Fucking traffic," I growl. Gripping the wheel tightly in my hands, I whisper, "I'm coming, Angel. Just hang on a little longer."

CHARLI   36

Tears pour down my face as I lie here trapped. The pain in my abdomen isn't as bad as it was earlier but it's still there. Every time I look down, I see all the blood that I've lost and more tears fall. There's so much blood. I'm sure there's no way that munchkin could have survived. She's a fighter but I don't think she will survive this, because I don't think I will. I'm going to die here trapped. Alone. And pinned under a chair.

As I lie here, a vision of Nic appears before me and I realize that he's my everything. I hope he lives a full and happy life without me and munchkin. Nic will never know how much I've truly fallen for him. I fell so hard for that man, he came into my life when I didn't even know I needed him. "I love you, Nic," I whisper, as a guttural sob breaks free at the thought of never seeing him again. I cup my belly with my free arm and I cry.

My self-pity moment is interrupted when I hear a commotion upstairs, followed by a lone gunshot.

My eyes widen.

Fear builds within.

I hold my breath waiting.

I'm frozen and then I hear, "Charli, Angel, where are you?"

"Nic," I whisper. "Nic," I shout a little louder but I'm so choked up with emotion that I can hardly speak. "Down here," I yell, but I don't think anyone can hear me. With all my might, I scream like I've never screamed before. "Niiiiiiiiiic!"

"I'm coming, Angel," he yells, and then the door above slams opens. Footsteps pound down the stairs; I can't see who it is but I know it's him, "Charli," he yells, "I'm here." He flies down the stairs and his eyes widen when he sees the blood and me trapped.

Sobs wrack through my body when my brain registers that he is here. He's really here. "You're here," I whisper, as he drops to his knees and stares down at me.

"Nic, help me. I'm…I…I think I lost the baby," I cry.

"Shhhh," he coos, as he brushes a tendril of hair off my face, "I'm here, Angel." He cups my face and looks lovingly at me. "I'm here," he repeats, his voice instantly soothing me.

"I'm gonna get you out of here," he says, "I've got you."

Leaning over me, he reaches behind me and unties my trapped arm. I collapse to the floor, wincing in pain when my shoulder connects with the cold cement. It was only a few inches but after being pinned in this position for a few hours, it felt like I fell off a cliff edge.

Rolling to my back, I take a deep breath at finally being free, but it doesn't ease any of the pain coursing through me right now. The room above me starts to spin. My vision blurs and everything around me becomes muffled. Nic is hovering above me, I can see his lips moving but I can't hear anything he's saying. All I can hear is a loud whooshing noise echoing in my head.

The last thing I see is Nic's gorgeous brown eyes staring at me before the darkness engulfs me.

When I open my eyes again, a bright light shining above causes me to close them quickly and groan.

From my side, Nic says, "Angel," and he squeezes my hand.

Turning my head toward the voice, I carefully open my eyes. "It's so bright," I whisper. He stands up and reaches over me. The sounds of a switch flicking vibrates through my head but the overhead lights turn off, leaving only a yellow glow from the wall behind me.

He sits back down and grips my hand and with the other, he runs his fingertips up and down my cheek. "Hi, Angel."

"Hi," I croak out. "Where am I?" I ask, everything is fuzzy and I can't remember why I'm here.

"You're in the hospital," he says. "Darren had you."

When he mentions Darren's name, my eyes widen and it all come crashing back to me. I pull my hand free from his and drop it to my stomach. I still have a slight pooch, "Munchkin?" I ask.

He stares at me, not saying a word, his silence is unnerving and then he smiles. "She's fine."

"Really?" My eyes widen at his words. He nods at me, "Really, really? Carter is okay?"

"Ohh, I love that name," a voice says from behind me. Turning my head, I see a group of people standing huddled together. My gaze flits over the group and then I realize my mom and dad are here. And so are Mr. and Mrs. Cruz, Abi, and Elena. I recognize them from photos Nic has around his place and Elena from my visit here when I was shopping with Bay.

"You're here?" I say, my eyes locked on Mom's.

"Of course," she says, pushing past Dad and walking over to me. "As soon as we got the call from Dominic, Dad and I jumped in the car and drove straight here." My eyes well with tears, Mom and Dad are here. Munchkin is fine and I'm safe.

I go to move my hand toward her to squeeze it but I wince in pain. Looking down I see my arm is in a sling and then I remember I was pinned. Turning my head back to Nic, I ask him the one question I'm not sure I want the answer to, "Where's Darren?"

"He's dead. Amanda shot him when we found you. He pulled a gun on us, she didn't hesitate and pulled the trigger."

"And Dean?" He doesn't get a chance to answer because the door to my room opens and Dr. Flynn Kelly walks in.

"Charli, you're awake," he says, as he walks to the end of my bed. He picks up my chart and looks over it. Lifting his gaze back to mine, he smiles. He really is good-looking, add in that sexy as hell accent and I can see why Avery fell for the dashing doctor.

He looks over to my family. "Can I ask you all to step out for a moment?"

They all nod and a chorus of "Glad you're okay," "We'll be back," and "I need coffee," can be heard as they all shuffle out. Nic stands too, bends down and kisses my forehead. "I'll be just outside."

Squeezing his hand, I shake my head. "Please stay."

He looks to Flynn and he nods. "That's fine by me."

The door closes behind our family and Flynn steps around to where Mom was standing. "How are you feeling, Charli?"

"Wiped," I tell him.

"That's to be expected. You have a dislocated shoulder and you suffered a placental abruption."

"What's that?" I ask, he's speaking English, I think, but I have no clue as to what a pla-thingy abruption is.

"A placental abruption is when the placenta partly or completely separates from the inner wall of the uterus. It occurs in one percent of pregnancies. It can occur at any time after twenty weeks. It's most common in the third trimester but I'd say the trauma of the last few days is the contributing factor to this happening to you now at just shy of twenty weeks."

"What does that mean for munchkin?"

"We will keep you in for the next few days so we can monitor you, since you are still bleeding quite heavily. You've already had one transfusion but at this stage, everything with the baby seems fine. Her heartbeat is strong and she's still wriggling around in there."

"What happens if I don't stop bleeding?"

"You'll need to discuss those plans with your OB, but from what I remember from my stint in maternity, we would get you past the thirty-four-week mark and then you'd have an emergency C-section to deliver the baby. You'd be administered medication needed to help your baby's lungs mature and to protect the baby's brain due to the early delivery. I've spoken with your OB and updated her of what recently transpired. I'll inform her that you're awake and she'll stop by to discuss the rest of your pregnancy."

"But right now, the baby is fine?" I question him, my hand hasn't left my stomach since he started talking.

"Baby is strong. She's a fighter, like her mom." He points to my shoulder. "We've popped your shoulder back in and you'll need the sling for a few days, but you will make a full recovery from that injury."

"Thanks, Dr. Kelly," I tell him, relieved that munchkin and I are okay.

"Please call me, Flynn."

Before we can discuss anything else, the door to my room swings open and Baylor barges in, Corey is close behind her. "Don't do that again, lady. I've been worried sick about you and BJ," she says, hugging me tightly. I wince from the pain in my shoulders but I can't really do much so I one-arm hug her back.

"Who's BJ?" Nic ask.

Bay turns to face him. She points at my stomach. "Baylor Junior," she says in a 'duh' tone of voice.

"We are not calling our baby BJ," Nic tells her.

"Well, what are you calling her then?" Baylor huffs, clearly annoyed we won't name our baby after her.

"Carter," Nic and I say in unison.

"I don't hate that," Bay tells us, "therefore I will allow it."

"Don't think you really have a choice, Kitten," Corey says, pulling Baylor into his chest. He whispers something into her ear and from the pink tinge that fills her cheeks and neck; I'm guessing it was something dirty.

"Glad you're okay," Bay says. Grabbing Corey's hand, she pulls him to the door, yes, he whispered something dirty to her. "I'll be back tomorrow with a billion cheese-burgers."

Before I can say anything, she and Corey are gone. If this was a cartoon, there'd be a Baylor and Corey shaped hole in the door to my hospital room.

"She really is something," Nic says to me.

Nodding my head I laugh. "You have no idea but she's my someone." Looking at him, I pat the mattress beside me. "But you're my number one so come snuggle with me."

"You sure? I don't want to hurt you."

"I'm sure." I shuffle over and try hide the discomfort on my face but I don't do a very good job. "I'll be fine, Nic. I need you to hold me."

"Well, when you put it like that, how can I resist?" He looks to Dr. Kelly. "Can I?"

"That's fine. I'll leave you for now but page me if you anything changes or if you have any questions."

Dr. Kelly turns and leaves my room and Nic climbs onto the bed. Carefully we maneuver ourselves so I'm snuggled into his side without injuring my shoulder, or Carter.

"You really sure we want to call her Carter?" I ask him.

"Yep, Carter Davis is a badass name."

"You mean, Carter Cruz is a badass name," I tell him. I press a kiss to his chest. "One day we will all be Cruzes," I say. My eyes become heavy and I drift off to sleep in Nic's arms. Our baby is safe and everything is right in the world again.

DOMINIC 37

After her ordeal with Darren, Charli spent two weeks in hospital. The bleeding from the placental abruption stopped after ten days and our doctor agreed that if Charli promised to stay off her feet, she'd be allowed to go home for the rest of the pregnancy, as long as no other complications arise. And by home, I mean my place. I managed to convince Charli to move in with me…

…We're lying together in Charli's tiny hospital bed, My Angel is asleep and wrapped around me like a monkey. Even though I'm uncomfortable, I wouldn't be anywhere else in this world. It's been ten sleepless nights but knowing that Charli and Carter are safe, I don't care that I'll need to see a chiropractor for the rest of my life. Their safety and happiness is all that matters to me.

Dr. Clark told us that Charli can go home in a few days, if she promises to take it easy and stay off her feet—ha, I can't see that happening—you've met Charli Davis, she doesn't know the meaning of taking it easy. I'm one-million-percent sure that my Angel would have agreed to anything to be able to go home, and I'm not ashamed to admit that I totally took advantage of this scenario. When this situation arose, operation 'Get Charli to Move In' commenced.

Knowing that I'd need reinforcements for this, I called in June and Frank, Charli's parents, to help me convince her that this was the best option, for her, the baby, and me. Surprising to me, they agreed that this was the best plan, even going so far as offering to help move her in.

If I thought asking them to help with convincing their daughter to move in was hard, I can only imagine what it will be like when I ask for their permission to marry her, because that's totally in the cards...and soon. Charli Davis is it for me. My heart and soul belong to her, I think they have from the moment my eyes landed on her in the bar just a few short months ago.

So with their approval, I am waiting for the right moment to ask. "I can hear your brain thinking from here, what's on your mind, Biker Boy?"

A chuckle breaks free. "You haven't called me Biker Boy in a while."

"I was dreaming about your bike, I can't wait to jump on again."

"Not 'til after Carter is born. You heard Dr. Clark, you need to take it easy."

"Sitting on a bike IS taking it easy."

"You and I both know that it's never just sitting on that bike. It leads to fucking on said bike, and as much as it pains me to say, there will be no bike fucking, or fucking in general, until our little munchkin safely arrives."

"No fucking, that's a bit much, don't you think?"

"Nope, I've read up on placental abruptions and we are so

lucky that you didn't go into labor. I'm not risking Carter for the sake of a fuck. We will have the rest of our lives to fuck, I think we can manage for a few months without."

She groans, "Ugh, you are so mean to me."

"Fucking is not in the cards, Agent Davis, but I never said anything about my tongue."

She lifts her head to stare at me. "I like that plan…think I can get a tongue preview?"

This is the perfect opening to drop my request, "I might be able to oblige but I need you to agree on one thing first."

"And what is your one request? You know I'll pretty much agree to anything to get your tongue between my thighs."

"I'm counting on that."

She lifts herself up farther. "I'm intrigued now so, Biker Boy, what is your condition?"

"Move in with me?"

Her eyes widen. "Come again?"

"I want you to move in with me. I want you, me, and Carter to be one big happy family under one roof."

"It's too soon."

"Angel, we are about to have a baby together, I think the soon boat has sailed."

"Are you sure?"

Nodding my head, I take her hands in mine. "I've never been more sure of anything. Charli Davis," dropping her hands, I cup her cheek, "I'm truly, madly, deeply in love with you, and you agreeing to move in will make me the happiest man in the world."

She nods her head. "Nic Cruz, you are my everything and I would love to move in with you. I love you to infinity and beyond. Now take me home and give me your tongue."

"We have to wait for the doctor's clearance but I promise, as soon as we are given the all clear, my tongue is yours."

Charli clearly really wants my tongue because later that day, she manages to sweet talk Dr. Clark into letting her out. I swear this woman could sell ice to Eskimos. It's really hard to say no to her but I don't mind at all because she's coming home…with me!

…and now here we are, but rather than following doctor's orders, Charli is gallivanting around the city. When I found Charli's note telling me she'd gotten an Uber to go and see Dean, I was furious. I had never felt anger like this before. She was just released from hospital and is meant to be on bed rest but no, my fierce baby momma is still playing super agent.

Leaning against my car, I fold my arms and wait for her to exit. I feel her before I see her. Looking up, I smile when I see her step outside and like she does after each prison visit, she looks to the sky and takes a calming deep breath. Prisons give her the heebie-jeebies, which is funny since in our line of work we visit them quite often.

She looks over and when she sees me, she's smiles but that smile drops when she sees the angry scowl on my face. Walking toward me, she's smiling, trying to placate me, but my anger must be showing on my face because her eyes show hesitation.

"Hey, what are you doing here?" she says, leaning into me to give me a kiss, but I turn my head and she kisses my cheek.

"More to the point, what are YOU doing here? You're supposed to be *home*. On bed rest."

"I needed to see Dean. I needed him to look me in the eye and confess everything."

"And you couldn't do that via FaceTime? Skype? Zoom? There's this thing called technology."

"Don't you dare sass me, Dominic Cruz." Shit, she called me Dominic, she's just as pissed as I am. "I'm pregnant, Nic. I'm not a damsel in distress who's made of glass. I needed to see him. I needed to hear everything from him. I needed closure so I can move forward and focus on munchkin. And you."

"And do you have your closure now?"

"Yes," she nods. "It's all closed and locked away, never to be actioned again." She reaches up and cups my cheek, just from her touch, the anger begins to dissipate. "I appreciate the concern but I'm fine. Really. Now take me home and get me five cheeseburgers along the way."

I want to be mad but she has a way of charming me, it's one of the many things I love about this woman. "You are lucky I love you, Charli Davis."

"You bet your fine ass I'm lucky and I promise from this moment on, I will stay home in bed...naked."

"Don't taunt me like that, woman, you know I can't ravage you like I want until after this baby is born."

"Weeell, we—"

"Nope, no hanky-panky 'til munchkin is born. I need you both healthy and safe." Raising my hand, I wiggle my fingers. "I'll be fine with Mrs. Palmer for the next few months."

"What about me?" Shrugging my shoulders, she pouts and it's totally adorable. "You are just mean, mister, taunting a bedridden pregnant woman like that."

Leaning into her, I whisper, "If you play your cards right and behave...in bed...with clothes on, I'll sweet talk the doctor at our next check up and get permission to ravage you, if AND when she deems it safe for you both."

"You better, Biker Boy. Now, since we can't get down

and dirty, get me my cheeseburgers, that's the next best thing right now."

Placing a chaste kiss on her lips, I open the car door and drive her to the nearest McDonald's, where she eats an insane number of cheeseburgers before I take her home and we snuggle—fully clothed—in bed with my hand resting on her tummy.

We've just hit the thirty-six week mark and Charli is glowing. Dr. Clark is amazed that we, well Charli, has made it this far, but my girls are fighters, there's no stopping them.

Lifting my head, I rest it in my palms and watch her sleep—hey, it's not creepy when I do it. She really is the most beautiful woman in the world, add in her pregnant glow and I'm speechless.

"Are you watching me sleep again?"

"Maybe," I tell her.

"No maybe, baby, I can feel your gaze on me."

"Is that so?" I say, running the tip of my finger down her cheek. Her eyes open and land on mine. She smiles and like always, it hits me in the chest and brings me alive like never before.

"Mmmhmpf, but I'd much rather feel something else."

"And what might that be?" I ask, trailing my finger down her neck.

"Your tongue..."

"What about my tongue?" I tease back, sliding my finger between her breasts that since becoming pregnant have increased in size, and I'm not complaining one bit.

"I need it…" she pants, when I lean forward and suck on her nipple through her silky nightgown.

"Need it where?" Rolling her to her back, I climb between her legs and kiss down her stomach. Dr Clark gave the all clear two weeks ago for us to get down and dirty, but there has been no bike or crazy wild monkey sex. There has been lots of tongues and fingers, I will not do anything to hurt Charli or the baby.

"A little farther," she mewls, pushing my head down.

Situating myself between her thighs, I push her night-gown up and I blow on her. "Niiiiiiic," she moans, "please."

"Patience, my Angel,"

She lifts her head and due to her stomach, I only see her eyes but they are firing daggers at me right now. Before she gets any angrier, I lean down and nuzzle my nose along her panty-covered slit, giving her want she wants.

"Yes," she pants, gripping my hair in her fingers, pulling on the strands. "More," she demands and from the breathiness of her words, I can tell she's on edge. Pushing the material of her panties to the side, I lick her from taint to clit, giving her what she wants. "Yeeeeesssss," she hisses, as I assault her slit with my tongue.

Nibbling on her clit, I slip a finger inside. Her walls clench around my digit, twisting around, I hit that magical spot deep within. Charli moans loudly when I suck hard on her clit and wriggle my fingers inside her. She saturates my face with her release. "Nic," she says and from the tone of her voice, the pleasure zone she was in only moments ago has disappeared, "my water just broke."

CHARLI 38

"I FUCKING HATE YOU," I SCREAM AT NIC. "YOU AND YOUR dick are never coming near my vagina again."

I've been in labor for five hours now, Dr. Clark agreed that I can try but right now, I wish I'd taken the C-section option. I have never felt pain like this before and I'm going all crazy psycho lady and taking it out on Nic. The contraction passes and then I begin to cry. "I'm sorry, Nic. Please don't hate me."

"Shhhh, Angel, it's fine."

"It's not fine," I snap, "I'm being a Baylor."

"Angel, you are about to push a watermelon out of your vagina, you can Baylor away."

"Charli," Dr. Clark interrupts us, "you are only two centimeters dilated, you need to start thinking about going for a C-section. With your abruption and the slow labor, I have concerns." My eyes widen when she says the word concerns.

"Concerns how? Is Carter okay? What's wrong?"

"Everything is fine, for now," she reassures me, "but I would really like you to consider a C-section. If we can prepare it will be less rushed and much easier for both you and the baby, BUT if you want to keep trying, we can. I'll have the team on standby for an emergency one, but I would like to avoid that if we can."

"Do it," I say without thinking.

"Are you sure?" Nic asks.

Looking to him, I nod my head, and sadly smile. "Yes, I'm sure. I'm tired and it hurts. I don't think I can do this."

"You can do this," Nic encourages.

"I can't…I just want to hold our little girl." Looking to Dr. Clark, I reaffirm, "Let's do it."

No sooner do I say those three words and it's all go-go-go. I'm wheeled into the operating room. Nic is whisked off to scrub up—FYI, he looks hot in scrubs. A needle is shoved into my spine, numbing me from the waist down —and let me tell you—it's the weirdest sensation ever. You can't feel what they are doing but you can sense what's happening.

Before we know it, the most magical cry rings through the room and Carter Cruz takes her first breath, well, screech. Holy crap on a cracker, can that little girl screech. I watch as Nic cuts the cord and then our lil' munchkin is whisked away to be checked over. Nic hovers next to the nurses doing their job and when one hands him our little girl, I burst into tears. The sight of him holding her will forever be etched into my mind.

He looks over at me and smiles. "Let me introduce you to your mommy," he says as he walks over to us. "She's the most beautiful woman in the world and, kid, you and I are lucky to have her on Team Cruz." He stops next to me. "Wanna hold your daughter?"

Nodding my head, he places her in my arms and as soon as I hold her, I'm instantly in love. I've heard other moms say that but I thought they were full of shit, but nope, it's one-billion-percent true. What I feel for Carter is unconditional ever-lasting love, much like my love for her daddy. As if he knows I'm thinking about him, Nic places a kiss on my temple. Looking up at him, he's grinning. "We did good, Daddy Cruz."

"Sure did, Momma Cruz."

Our Hallmark family moment is interrupted when Dr. Clark informs me that I'm being transferred to recovery. Nic and Carter can come too and I'm thankful for that, I don't want to ever be away from her. It's only been a few moments but I'm addicted to her. Everything about her is perfect. Her button nose. Her chubby cheeks—probably from eating too many cheeseburgers. Her full head of dark hair and her eyes. Her eyes are a mirror image of mine, just in mini form.

After spending a few hours in recovery I'm finally transferred to my room. I spent a long time there as I had some bleeding in relation to the placenta rupture. With medication, oxytocin, and some abdominal massaging, we got my uterus to contract and the bleeding stopped, saving me from having to have a D&C, dilation and curettage, surgery.

There's a knock at my door and Elena pokes her head in. "Hey," she says with a smile. Her eyes drop to the bundle of joy in my arms. "How's my niece doing?"

"She's perfect," Nic proudly says. He's been sporting the biggest smile since Carter was placed into his arms. He pouted, yes pouted, when he had to give her to me so I could feed her. As soon as Carter finished feeding, he swooped in and took hold of her again.

"You're going to have to put her down sometime soon," I tell him. I look to Elena. "He's had her in his arms since she was born."

"Aww, is my big brother a softie? Does wee lil' Carter have you wrapped around her teeny tiny little finger already?"

"Yep, and I don't care. Carter Cruz is the most beautiful baby in the world," he proudly declares, as he looks over to me and adds, "Just like her mommy is the most beautiful angel in the entire universe."

"Ohh my God," Elena whines, "shoot me now. When did you grow a vagina?"

"Don't say that word around her," Nic says, cupping Carter's ear.

Elena and I both laugh at him but if I'm honest, it's sexy as fuck seeing Nic in dad mode.

⎯ⅲⅲⅲ◯◯ⅲⅲⅲⅲⅲⅲⅲⅲⅲ⎯

We are finally home from hospital after a five-night stay. Nic and I are watching Carter sleep. Who knew a sleeping baby could be so entertaining? Sliding my arm around Nic's waist, I snuggle in. He presses a kiss to my head and whispers, "Marry me?"

My head snaps up and I stare into his eyes, from what I see reflecting back at me, he means it and without missing a beat, I whisper back, "Yes."

"Really?" he says, spinning me around to face him. He cups my cheeks in his palms. "You really will marry me?"

Nodding my head, I smile. "Yes. A thousand times yes."

He lowers his hands to my waist and lifts me up

hugging and kissing me. It's romantic but at the same time, so painful. I wince and groan in pain. "Ohh crap," he says, lowering me to my feet. "I'm so sorry, Angel."

"It's fine, we got caught up in the moment. Now, where's my ring?"

He grabs my hand and drags me out of Carter's nursery and into our room. He pulls open his underwear drawer and digs into the back. He pulls out a Tiffany blue box and turns to face me. With a smirk on his face, he drops to one knee and takes my left hand. "Charli Davis, will you do me the honor of becoming my wife?"

Nodding my head, my eyes well with tears and I blubber, "Yes. Yes I'll marry you."

He pulls out the ring I've been admiring online, it has a diamond platinum band with a square mixed-cut diamond and slips it onto my left hand. Lifting my hand, I inspect the ring. It's everything I wanted and more. Looking down to my fiancé, I cup his cheek in my palm, the diamond on my finger sparkling in the afternoon light. Leaning down, I press my lips to his. Resting my forehead on his, I whisper, "I'm yours forever, Nic, and I cannot wait to officially start our life together."

DOMINIC 39

IN A FEW SHORT DAYS, CHARLI WILL OFFICIALLY BECOME MRS. Cruz and I cannot wait for us to officially become a family, well, in the eyes of the law official. We were a family as soon as those two pink lines appeared on all six tests Charli took.

The last few months, since Carter arrived, have been one crazy roller coaster but I would not change one single thing. Who knew someone so cute and cuddly could A. Scream as loud as she does, B. Poop so much, and C. Projectile vomit. If projectile vomiting was a sport, she'd win hands down. Actually, I'd change the vomiting. Poop and pee, easy-peasy, but vomit, yeah nah, I'd rather have a root canal.

Tonight I have arranged a special date for my Angel. It will be our first night time away from Carter but I plan to keep Charli in such an orgasmically blissed state that she won't notice. Aunty Bay and Uncle Corey are having Carter for the night. Charli is packing her overnight bag and I'm changing her. "Now, my lil' munchkin," I say to her, "please poop lots for Aunty Bay and if you can have a number three explode over her while you are in her arms again, that'd be great." A chuckle breaks free when I remember the first time Carter did a number three and Bay happened to be the recipient, and so far, the only recipient of one.

"Did you just ask our daughter to shit on Bay?" Charli questions from the doorway. Looking up, I see my Angel standing in the entrance to Carter's room staring at me. She's wearing a navy sundress that hugs her curves and showcases her gorgeous tits. Charli always had nice tits but her tits since having Carter are even more plump and delectable.

"Yep," I say, letting the 'P' pop. "If anyone deserves to be shit upon, it's your best friend. Don't get me wrong, she's great but..." I shrug, leaving that sentence open-ended. Looking back down at our giggling munchkin, I grin when I see a twinkle in her eye that I take as her confirming that she'll shit on Bay for me. "That's my girl," I tell her, bopping her on the tip of her nose.

Charli shakes her head at me. "You are terrible, Agent Cruz."

"I'll show you just how terrible I am as soon as we're alone." Picking up our daughter, I wink at my Angel and notice her cheeks darken. She's biting her lip in that 'fuck me now way' and she's clenching her thighs together, from that action I know, tonight is going to be fucking—literally—amazing.

We've just said goodbye to Carter, Charli seems a little sad but I'm sure a soon as we get home, I can get her mind off our daughter. Reaching over, I rest my hand on her knee and squeeze. She covers my hand, I can feel her gaze on me. "What's on your mind, Angel?"

"Is it silly that I miss her already?"

"Not at all." I glance at her and smile, turning my attention back to the road. "I miss her too, but I promise that I'll do my best to keep you and your mind occupied."

"And what do you have in mind?"

"I cannot reveal all my secrets to you...but I will say, I'm ever so glad you're wearing a dress."

"And why is that?"

"For starters, I can do this." Sliding my hand up her thigh, I slip it between the gap. She widens her legs for me and I run the tip of my finger up her panty-covered slit. She shudders and I can't help but grin, but I'm also cursing myself. We are still ten minutes from home and just from running my finger over her panties, they're soaked and my cock is now rock-hard.

"And then what?" she breathlessly says. Pressing on my hand and pushing my palm against her heated mound.

"And then nothing." Her eyes widen and she shoots daggers at me. "Nothing because if I keep going, I will either crash or pull over and fuck you on the side of the road, and for what I have planned, I don't want any interruptions."

"Well, hurry up and get home, because I need you now, Nic."

She doesn't need to tell me twice, so I increase my speed and make the remaining ten-minute trip in seven. We pull into the garage and I turn the car off. Turning to face Charli, I find her staring intently at me. We both lean forward at the same time and our lips slam together in a heated and carnal kiss. I thread my fingers into her hair and deepen our connection. Her tongue licks along my lips before slipping into my mouth. The temperature in the car rising with each lash of our tongues together.

"More," she moans against my lips.

Breaking the connection, I pull back and stare. Charli is gorgeous at the best of times but when she's glowing with arousal, fuck me sideways, she's stunning. Her cheeks are flushed, her chest rapidly rising and falling with each breath. "Don't move," I growl at her. Pressing a kiss to the tip of her nose, I pull back, unbuckle my belt, and climb out. I round the hood of the car and open her door. Staring down at her, I offer my hand. She places her palm in mine and an electrical current zaps through me, every nerve ending in my body buzzing with desire.

Pulling her up, I slide my hand around her waist and pull her in. Grazing my nose up her neck, I nibble her earlobe and whisper, "I'm going to fuck you on my bike and then we are going to take a ride. When we arrive home, I'll fuck you on the bike again and then I'm going to feed you. Then I'll carry you to our bed and I'm going to make love to my fiancée all night long." Lifting my head, I stare at my Angel. "Nod if you agree with this plan."

Her tongue darts out and she licks her lip. She nods her head, steps around me, and walks over to my bike. Along the way, she lifts her dress over her head, leaving her in her panties and bra. She looks at me over her shoulder and drops her dress to the cement. She spins to face me, and walks backward to my back. She lifts herself up onto the seat and spreads her legs. She leans back on her hands and stares at me intently. Raising her eyebrows she seductively says, "What are you waiting for, Biker Boy?"

"Abso-fucking-lutely nothing." Stalking toward her, I grip the collar of my shirt and pull it over my head, stopping between her spread legs.

"Man, it's hot when you do that."

"Do what?" I ask, as I unbutton my jeans.

"Remove your shirt with one hand like that."

"Duly noted." I kick off my jeans and briefs. My cock springs free, the tip glistening with arousal at the sight of a lingerie-clad Charli on my bike.

"I stand corrected," she says, her eyes roaming over my naked body, "you fully naked is the hottest sight ever."

"You in lingerie on my bike is the hottest thing ever."

We stare at one another and like in the car moments ago, the temperature in the garage increases with each passing moment. Charli lifts her hand and drags the tip of her finger down her chest and under her panties. "I stand corrected, you on my bike in lingerie with your hand in your panties is the hottest sight ever."

With my eyes locked on Charli, I take the final step toward her and I slide my hand into her panties with hers. Together we slide our fingers in and out of her slit. The material of her panties is in the way; pulling my hand out, I grip the side and tear them off her body. Dropping to my knees, I nudge her hand out of the way with my nose, and inhale before licking her from taint to clit. "Niiiiiic," she moans. Gripping my head in her hands, she presses my face into her mound as I begin to lick up and down her slit. Pushing my tongue inside, she moans, thrusting herself against my tongue. I slip a finger inside, pulling out, I thrust back in and it sets her off, she orgasms—loudly—and coats my face with her arousal.

When her body tremors cease, I kiss up her body. Her skin breaking out in goosebumps. Kissing up her neck, I lift her leg, and wrap it around my waist. Lifting my head, I gaze into her hazel orbs as I press my length inside her, her head drops back as I slide myself in to the hilt.

"Watch," I growl, she lifts her head and together we watch my dick slide in and out. Thrusting my hips back and forth, in and out. We rock ourselves into oblivion, both of us crashing over the edge at the same time. Murmuring each other's name as pleasure courses through our veins.

Resting my forehead against hers, I vow, "I love you, Charli Davis."

"I love you too."

It's the middle of the night and Charli and I are naked in bed, she's cuddled into my side and is sound asleep. We did exactly as I planned and now we are both exhausted, well fucked, but exhausted. I lost count as to how many orgasms I gave my Angel, but the image of her fingering herself on my bike will be engrained in my memory forever.

Brushing a tendril of hair behind her ear, I stare down at her. She really is beautiful, and lives up to her name of Angel. She's pure on the inside and out. I'm still amazed that she's mine. Sure, our journey here hasn't been easy but anything worth fighting for is worth it, and I would go to hell and back for her, and Carter. Those two own my heart and soul.

"Are you staring at me again?" she asks, lifting her head to look up at me.

"Yep, I can't help it."

"You are too sweet but if you don't get some shut-eye now, tomorrow with our lil' munchkin is going to be tough."

"It will be worth it. You are worth every sleepless moment."

"You are such a sweet talker and I love it, but we need sleep."

"Fine," I huff, "but in the morning…"

"…we can do it on your bike again before we go get Carter."

"I was going to suggest waffles but I'm okay with another bike fucking."

"Waffles on the bike," she suggests.

"Charli on the bike…waffles off Charli in the kitchen."

"I like that plan." She presses a quick kiss to my lips. "Now sleep."

She snuggles into my side and like she always does, she drifts off to sleep in my arms. This is the best way to fall asleep, and I'm lucky because I get to do this every day for the rest of my life. I'm one lucky son of a bitch.

CHARLI 40

TODAY IS MY WEDDING DAY AND I'LL OFFICIALLY BECOME Mrs. Biker Boy. I cannot wait to start my life with Nic and Carter officially as a Cruz.

Staring at my reflection in the mirror, I think back to when I first met Nic and my heart flutters, just like it did that night when I saw him pull up on his bike at Bin 501. I was never into the biker boy thing, but that night I did many things I'd never done before, and I'm glad I took the chance because it led me here.

A knock on the door startles me. "Come in," I yell.

"I can't," a deep gruff sexy voice says through the wood, "it's bad luck to see the bride but I needed to see you."

Walking over to the door, I rest my palm flat against the surface. "Well how can you see me, if there's a door in the way?"

"I can feel your presence whenever you're around." *Swoon.*

"You've already sealed the deal, Biker Boy, no need to go all out with the swoon."

"I will swoon you like you've never been swooned before, Angel. Now, in the front pocket of your overnight bag is a little something for you."

Walking over to my bag, I unzip the pocket and inside is a long black box. "What did you do?" I ask.

"Open it and see."

Lifting the lid, I gasp. Inside the box is a Pandora bracelet with three charms: baby booties with a pink stone, a motorcycle, and last but not least, a rose gold infinity heart dangle charm.

"Nic," I cry, "it's beautiful."

"Just like you. Carter and I cannot wait to see you, now dry those tears and come marry me."

Nodding, I stand here and stare at the bracelet when I hear Baylor yelling, "Dominic Cruz, what are you doing here? You better not have seen her."

"Calm your tits, woman, I stayed in the hallway this whole time."

"You better not be lying to me. I don't care that it's your wedding day, I will kick you in the nuts if you ruin this for my girl in there."

Swinging the door open, Baylor lifts her hand and covers Nic's eyes, even though his back is to me. "He can't see you," she growls at me over his shoulder.

Pushing Baylor's hands out of the way, I cover his eyes with my hands and step in front of him. I press my lips to his. "I love the bracelet." KISS "I love you." KISS "And I cannot wait to marry you." KISS

"I love you too, Angel, and I cannot wait for you to officially be mine."

"Seriously," Baylor growls. "You," she pulls on my arm

and covers Nic's eyes, "inside, and you, get to the altar so you can make her yours."

"Yes, ma'am."

"Don't fucking call me ma'am," she growls at Nic, and I can't help but laugh.

"Watch your mouth, Kitten," Corey snarls from behind her and I laugh again. I notice Bay's eyes glaze over when she hears Corey's voice. "Sorry to break up this Hallmark moment, but it's go time, people."

"See you soon, fiancé," I whisper into Nic's ear. "I'll be the one in a white dress."

"And I'll be in the one in a tux with his eyes glued to you."

Corey drags Nic away from me and Baylor pushes me back into the dressing room. "Seriously, I leave you alone for five minutes and you do this."

"Well, you shouldn't have snuck off to fuck you husband in the room next door."

"How did you know?" she asks, as she attaches my veil.

"I have ears and you're not all that quiet when you come. I see nothing has changed since the WitSec cabin with you two."

"You're just jealous that I got some just now and you have to wait until after the ceremony."

"Touché," I tell her, but really I'm fine because last night before Nic took off, he and I had one last romp on his bike. Doing it on his bike is one of my favorite extracurricular activities to partake in. Taking a deep breath, I run my hand down my dress and stare at myself again.

Looking over to my best friend I proudly say, "Let's go get me married."

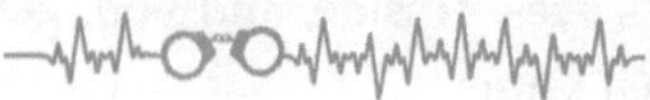

I am now officially Charli Cruz; we are the Cruzes. I love saying that just as much as I love my husband and our daughter. Carter is in Nic's arms and we are walking back down the aisle as a family. I'm grinning from ear to ear, I have never been happier than I am in this moment.

Looking up at my husband—love saying that already—and daughter, my grin widens. Happiness, love, and everything in between courses through my veins. Falling for Agent Cruz was the best decision I ever made.

EPILOGUE

Charli

…three years later

Watching Nic in a pink tutu with Carter in her orange one has my ovaries bursting at the seams, if I wasn't already pregnant, I'm sure I would be. Nic is the best dad and he treats our little princess like a queen. I can't wait to see what he's like with our little princes, Davis and DJ—Dominic Jr.—when they arrive in a few short weeks.

A few weeks ago we moved into our forever home. With twins on the way, the old place wasn't big enough for a family of five but this place, it's big enough for a football team but after DJ and Davis, no more kids for us. Carter is already a handful, so I can only imagine what my two new Cruzes are going to be like when the three of them are together.

Nic and Carter are still in the living room dancing

around together. If I wasn't the size of our new house, I'd be up with them, but instead I'm sitting on our new blue sofa eating, you guessed it, cheeseburgers. The burger craving from having twins is out of control, thank the heavens for twenty-four seven McDelivery.

"No eating on the sofa, Mommy," Carter says.

"I think Mommy gets a free pass," Nic says, scooping her up into his arms and flying her around the room. "Growing babies is hard work, so we need to make things as easy as possible for Mommy until the boys arrive."

"Okay, Daddy," she says. "Can we go for a swim?"

"If you have a nap, sure."

"Put me down," she says to Nic, she races over to me and grips my cheeks. "Daddy said if I nap, I can go swimming so I'm going to nap."

"Okay, munchkin. Do you want me to tuck you in?"

"No, I'm a big girl now, I do it." She rests her hands on my big belly and gets close, then she whispers, "I'm going to nap, baby boys, and then swim." She kisses my stomach and my eyes well with tears at the scene before me. Damn pregnancy hormones making me emotional at the drop of a hat.

Sitting here, I watch Carter skip to her room. "We did good, didn't we?" Nic says, taking a seat next to me and pulling me into his side.

Nodding my head, I wipe away a stray tear. "We sure did." Leaning my head back, I stare up at him and I'm overcome with emotion. "I really am a lucky woman and I'm so glad I climbed on the back of your bike that night."

"Me too, Angel, me too." He kisses my temple and drapes his arm over my belly. Snuggling into him, I pull his arm tighter around me and sigh. #TeamCruz really is the best team to be on, and I can't wait for our trio to become a quintuple.

THE END!

BONUS EPILOGUE

Charli

...nineteen years later

"I CAN'T BELIEVE OUR LITTLE GIRL IS GRADUATING COLLEGE today," I say to Nic, as he steps out of the bathroom. A towel around his waist with his abs on display, rendering me speechless when my gaze drops to the illusive 'V.' Nic is just as good-looking today as he was twenty-two years ago when we first met.

The doorbell rings, snapping my attention away from the dirty thoughts that were playing through my mind at the sight of my husband semi-naked. "I'll get it, you," I twirl my finger at him, "put some clothes on."

"You don't tell me to do that often," he teases with a wink.

"Down, boy. We cannot be late for our daughter's college graduation."

"Spoilsport," he whines, dropping his towel and giving me an unobstructed view of his sexy as sin body.

"I was going to say maybe when we get home we can go for a ride, if you know what I mean, but if you're going to be like that…"

He grabs my arm and pulls me into his chest. "We are definitely going for a ride later, Mrs. Cruz."

"I'll hold you to that, Biker Boy."

He presses his lips to mine and what starts out as a sensual kiss, quickly turns heated. The doorbell rings again, pulling us apart.

"Coming," I yell, as I walk away from Nic to answer the door.

"You will be later," he teases as I close the door behind me. Walking down the hallway, I open the door to see Mason, Avery and Flynn's son and Carter's boyfriend, standing in the doorway.

"Hey, Mase," I greet him. "I thought you'd be with Carter?"

"I…I…I wanted to talk to you and Mr. Cruz before the ceremony."

"Okay, come on in. Nic is just getting ready."

"Can I get you a drink?" He shakes his head. "You look nervous, is everything okay?" He nods his head, sweat beading at this temple.

"Mason, what are you doing here?" Nic says, walking into the living area doing up the cuff on his dress shirt.

"I wanted to speak with you and Mrs. Cruz."

"How many times have we told you, it's Dominic and Charli."

"Okay, Dominic and Charli, I wanted to speak to you both."

"Is everything okay?" I ask him, he looks like he's going to throw up.

"Yeah, I'm just nervous."

"Why are you nervous, son?" Nic asks him. I have a sneaking suspicion I know why he's here but my loving husband is clueless.

"I wanted to ask you both something."

"Okay, what did you want to ask?" I offer, hoping my tone will ease the poor boy's nerves.

"As you know, your daughter and I have been seeing each other for a few years now." Carter and Mason have been seeing each other since we went to Bora Bora for Avery and Flynn to renew their wedding vows three years ago. Seems our kids got caught up with the love associated with the trip, and when we returned, they were glued at the hip and have been together ever since. "Well, I love your daughter very much and I want your blessing to ask her to marry me."

Bringing my hands to my lips, my eyes well with tears at the sweetness coming from him. I look to Nic and I notice he's clenching his teeth. As I watch him, I have no idea if he'll be okay with this. Carter is his baby girl, her getting engaged means her daddy is no longer her number one, but what he doesn't know is, a girl's daddy is always her number one. I know mine is.

"You want to marry my daughter?" he asks, I internally giggle at his use of my and not our.

"Yes, sir. I love her more than anything and I want to spend the rest of my life with her."

"She's my baby, I can't just give her to the first person who comes asking."

"Nic," I chide and scowl at him.

"I understand, sir, but there is no one out there who

will love her like I do. I will treat her like the princess she is and I'll give her anything and everything I can."

Nic stares at Mason. The poor boy is shaking in his boots. "You ever hurt her, and I will end you. I don't care that your father is one of my best friends. I will end you if my daughter ever sheds one tear because of you."

"No sir, only happy tears, unless we're watching *The Notebook*, those tears I have no control over."

Nic out stretches his hand. "Welcome to the family, son."

"I need her to say yes first."

"She will," Nic reassures him. "She loves you like I love her mother but remember my warning."

He nods. "I'll remember but I will never hurt her. My dad would be in line after you to kick my ass to Ireland and back."

"Looks like it will be a double celebration today," I excitedly say. "I better organize more champagne for the celebration afterward."

The doorbell rings again and I walk over, answering it, I smile when I see Avery and Flynn standing there. Grinning. Seems these two were privy to what Mason was here to ask us. "Looks like we will officially be family."

"Looks like it," Avery says, pulling me in for a hug. When she pulls back she has a look in her eye.

"Why do I get the feeling you know something I don't know?"

"Boy do I have the gossip of all gossip for you," she excitedly says. Linking arms with Avery, I pull her inside, Flynn follows. "Lily and Clay eloped and are pregnant."

Pausing midstep, my eyes open wide as I process her words. "Come again? Did you just say Lily Cox and Clay Knight are married?"

"Yep," Avery confirms. "Bay and Cress are now officially family."

Baylor and Cress are what you'd call frenemies. Those two love to pick at each other. It's quite entertaining to watch. "Holy shit," I say, "I better order extra tequila for later."

"Yep," she says, letting the 'P' pop. "Lots and lots of tequila will be needed."

"How did this happen?" I ask Avery.

"Seems those two have been sneaking around for a few months and when she discovered she was pregnant, they decided to fly to Vegas and get married."

"Lily really is a mini Bay. And I bet right now Bay is fuming."

"Actually, she took the news much better than I thought. Corey and Preston, on the other hand, not so much. They are both livid right now."

"I'd hate to be those kids at this moment," I say.

"I know, right?"

Holy shit, this day just got interesting and we haven't even left the house yet. I thought our daughter graduating was going to be the highlight but no, her boyfriend wants to propose, and my best friend is about to become a grandma and gained a son-in-law. Life with kids sure is interesting. I'm just glad that my three are the sane ones within our group.

"Angel, we need to get going, if we are late, Carter will kill us," Nic says, interrupting my thoughts.

"Okay, let me grab my purse and jacket."

Standing up, I grab my things. We stop at Elena's to pick up Elena, Davis, and DJ—they had a sleepover at their aunt's place last night—and then the five of us, make our way to Carter's graduation.

They day is perfect, surprise baby and wedding included.

Our little girl looked amazing up there on stage and now, she's a newly engaged woman. My heart is full right now. Watching my daughter fall in love and get her happily ever after is just as amazing as when I got mine all those years ago.

There is no better feeling than falling in love and getting to live your very own happily ever after with the one you love. I've got mine and so has my daughter. I just need my sons to get theirs and then my life will be perfect in every way possible.

I thank Dominic Cruz every single day for falling for me.

Nic walks over to me, he has a glint in his eye. "Mrs. Cruz," he croons, pulling me into his arms, pressing a kiss to my temple.

Looking up at my husband, I smile. "Take me home, Biker Boy."

"With pleasure."

Linking hands with my husband, we leave our friends and family to celebrate, while we celebrate in our own way at home, just the two of us.

To see how Avery and Flynn got together, grab Falling for
Dr. Kelly.

**Every force has an equal and opposite attraction.
Love being the most volatile of them all.**

AVERY
My life is anything but boring.
So what if I'm an introvert and prefer to focus on my career?
I was fine.
Until I met him—Flynn Kelly.
The doctor with the sexy Irish accent.
I thought we were unbreakable, until someone close hurts me
in an unimaginable way.
Can two opposites fight the laws of attraction or will it end up
tearing us apart?

FLYNN
I work hard, and play even harder.
When it came to women, I could have anyone I want.
Until I met her—Avery Evans.
She's quiet, shy, and everything I'm not.
But we're drawn together like magnets, sparking each other
to life.
When the unthinkable happens, our differences really show.
Is our attraction about to sizzle and flame out? Only time will
tell.

To find out what happens with Lexi, Preston and Cress, grab Falling for Dr. Knight.

falling for

Chaos and tragedy can either bring us together, or tear us apart.
Falling in love isn't like it is in fairy tales.

CRESSIDA
Being a single mom is hard.
But Lexi is my life, and I'll do anything for my daughter.
I just never expected tragedy to strike, or for my past to haunt us.
Or for Dr. Preston Knight to be the man who saves us.
The same man I should *never* have fallen in love with.

PRESTON
I'm the best in my field.
Being a doctor is in my *blood*.
My focus is always on my career.
Until her—Cressida Bayliss.
I've fought many battles, but never one so close to my heart.
This is the biggest fight of my life, and with my heart on the line, I can't afford to lose.

She's the twin you love to hate. Will Baylor get her HEA and redeem herself? Grab Falling for Agent Cox today and find out.

There's a fine line between love and hate.
And a love fueled from hate is the strongest of them all.

BAYLOR
My life hasn't gone as I planned, but it's all my doing.
I'm given a second chance.
But I didn't count on him—Agent Corey Cox.
He's on the straight and narrow, abiding by the rules.
He calms my inner beast and makes me want to be a better person.
When my past reappears, that wildness inside sparks to life again.
Is his love enough to stop me turning my back on everything I've worked so hard for?

COREY
I live my life by the book.
Being an agent is everything to me.
The lines are never blurred.

Until her—Baylor Evans.

She's wild, carefree, and marches to the beat of her own drum.

She brings out a side to me I never knew existed.

But it all implodes, when I'm faced with an impossible decision.

Either way I lose.

ACKNOWLEDGEMENTS

This is the final book in the Falling series and I'm sad to say goodbye to these characters. They have been my life for the last twelve months and I think I saved the best for last. I know **Z** has claimed Dominic as hers but he's mine. I fell hard for this man while I was writing him and he will always hold a special place in my heart.

I know you won't ever read this, but thank you **Sophia Bush** and **Josh Bowman** for being my muses. You helped bring Nic and Charli to life and make them the kick ass characters that they are…if its ever turned into a film, I want you two to play Charli and Nic.

My beta babes; **Andi, Stef, Lana, Bec** and **Tara;** thank you ladies once again for reading my book baby and giving me your opinions and feedback. You gals are rock stars and I would be lost without you.

My editor, **Karen**, from **Barren Acres Editing;** I'm running out of things to say. You're not only my editor, but you're also a great friend; why do you live so far away? Thank you, once again for helping me turn my book baby from a pile of crap into a beautiful book baby.

My cover designer, **Kristie** from **Vanilla Lily Designs**. As soon as I saw this cover, I knew it was Nic and Charli. With the little tweeks I asked for, you made it absolutely perfect and its gorgeous amongst the rest of the Falling books. Thank you for a gorgeous cover to round out the series.

To **Gem** from **Gems' Precise Proofreading** thank you for checking my I's are dotted and my T's are crossed. You were an absolute gem <— corny, I know, to work with.

To the following authors; **Alanda Jade, Chloe Renee, Corinne Mazille, Renee Linda, Anita Maxwell, Rebecca Barber, Leesa Bow, Tara Lee, Cass Fowler, Sophie Blue** and **Linda Higgins;** thank you for your support, encouragement and writing sprints. Without you guys, I'd be a mess in the corner drinking wine from my coffee mug.

To **my readers**, thank you for the kind words that you message me with each release. 9 out of 10 times, these arrive just when I need a pick me up and they always do. From the bottom of my heart, thank you for supporting me and my books.

And finally, **my family; Troy, Piper** and **Kade.** You three are my rocks, my loveable pains in the butt who push me to be the best. You are my everything. Love you all to the moon and back XoXoX

Cheers,
Dana Xo

ALSO BY DL GALLIE

STAND ALONES

Out of Nowhere

Antecedent

Seven Nights

Doc Steel

Christmas Treats

Oops

Fractured:A driven world novel - coming mid 2021

IPHTILY - coming late 2021

In the Dark of Night anthology**

Secrets anthology**

***only available in paperback direct from me*

FALLING NOVELS

Falling for Dr. Kelly

Falling for Dr. Knight

Falling for Agent Cox

Falling for Agent Cruz

The Liquor Cabinet: Series boxset

FACEBOOK ~ INSTAGRAM ~ BOOKBUB

GOODREADS ~ WEBSITE

dlgallieauthor@outlook.com

Sign up to my newsletter

ABOUT THE AUTHOR

DL Gallie is from Queensland, Australia, but she's lived in many different places all over the world, including the UK and Canada. She currently resides in Central Queensland with her husband and two munchkins. She and her husband have been together since she was sixteen, and although they drive each other crazy at times, she couldn't imagine her life without him.

Shortly after her son was born, DL began reading again. With encouragement from her husband, she picked up the pen and started writing, and now the voices in her head won't shut up.

DL enjoys listening to music, drinking white wine in the summer, red wine in the winter, and beer all year round. She's also never been known to turn down a cocktail, especially a margarita.